I0586755

JOURNEY TO YUWMAH

ANCIENT WISDOM FOR A BRIGHTER WORLD

JOHN SAOMES

Inspire Point
PUBLISHING

Inspire Point Publishing
PO Box 972
Beenleigh, Queensland 4207
Australia
Email: admin@inspirepointpublishing.com

 A catalogue record for this book is available from the National Library of Australia

NATIONAL
LIBRARY
OF AUSTRALIA

Designed by: Peta Hansford
Cover Illustration: Olivia Mills

Journey to Yuwmah: Ancient Wisdom for a Brighter World
[The Yuwmahn Compendium]
ISBN: 978-0-9942910-5-9

To Peta,
who inspired me to see further,
to aim higher,
and to dream bigger.

ANCIENT YUWMAHN CREDO

All to be mindful of others...
~ learn caring

All to help each other...
~ learn sharing

All to listen to parents...
~ learn respect

All to honour elders...
~ learn wisdom

All to speak quietly...
~ learn gentleness

All to be kind...
~ learn patience

All to find peace together...
~ learn love

PREFACE

Each member of the human family follows their own unique and personal journey through life. This book documents a telling fragment of one such journey. Through the eyes of the central characters we embark on a voyage of discovery: a reflection of the past, a reassessment of the present, and a re-evaluation of our future as the dominant species on planet Earth.

The point of this journey is to challenge the reader to consider the most significant philosophical questions facing mankind into the twenty-first century:

- What is the meaning and most noble purpose of life?
- What is the best way for mankind to live?
- How do we design the ideal world to maximise human happiness?
- How do we govern ourselves to enhance the human experience?

My purpose in writing this book is to promote a broad conversation about the nature of the world that is, and how we might fix the problems we've caused. By my reckoning, our earthly home is in a terrible condition, and it's our fault. By the unbridled greed of a few and the thoughtless inaction of the many, we've created a dangerous future for every living creature, including ourselves.

I am totally convinced that the current practices around the world are not sustainable—that there must be a bold departure from the present system of global governance and capitalist industrialisation if we are to survive.

Mankind needs a new and better way to live, with particular emphasis on maximising human happiness and enhancing the human experience, while protecting our planet and every form of life. As the author of the *Yuwmahn Compendium*, I submit the following Yuwmahn concepts for your consideration.

N.B. It is not my intention to pass judgement on anyone. The purpose of the dialogue among my central characters is to explore and document some of the arguments and options, and nothing more. Ultimately, the reader must make their own comparisons, draw their own conclusions, settle their own minds, and formulate their own values.

Together we can make the world better …

John Saomes

CHAPTER 1

I am Mahonri, son of Melesch and Tepa.
Welcome to Yuwmah!

Our tiny plane buzzed between snow-capped peaks and sheer cliffs, its wings possessed by a primitive and all-powerful urge to reach out and make contact. Through the course of the morning we had flown far from civilisation—so very far into the unknown.

I peered out through the icy window, teeth clenched as a dense layer of cloud draped over the mountaintops trapping us deep in the rugged gorges. The scenery was breathtaking—the experience overwhelming.

Wisps of frosty mist rose like faint ghosts against the timeless backdrop to meet the churning weather above. As I watched their haunting progress, my baffled brain struggled to understand how such splendour had remained hidden from the probing eyes of modern science for so long. Ours was a time in history when mankind boasted an intimate understanding of every earthly aspect, yet my exhaustive search of the world's greatest repositories of knowledge netted not a single jot or tittle of the magnificence before me. I could only conclude that we were the first humans to see these majestic wonders up-close.

For this reason I had once again chosen to travel halfway around the globe in search of an untold story. Ancient antiquities were the flavour of the month, so why wouldn't we follow the crowd and cash in on the new-found curiosities while there was an easy dollar to be made? After all, wasn't that what life was about?

My latest assignment was without doubt a once in a lifetime opportunity, even for a seasoned freelancer such as I. The usual risks and dangers associated with such madcap adventures weighed dimly, but the chance to be the first to explore a phenomenon surviving in isolation for thousands of years was a rare opportunity.

Our studies of satellite images from a remote region of South America showed a scattering of sizeable constructions strewn randomly through deep mountain passes.

"I want you to go and bring back a story," muttered my editor without emotion.

I smiled my acceptance, and with a brief nod the deal was struck. From the beginning, the support team met the project with spirited enthusiasm, looking forward to a few days of overseas travel with perks aplenty and a sizeable dose of adventure along the way.

Despite their excitement, I was well aware that a human-interest story such as this would barely make the evening news. In the grander scheme of things this entire exercise was probably destined to be little more than a low-key assignment, especially if we found nothing of significance.

As for me—initially I looked forward to a change of scenery, but as time wore on I was having second thoughts. I was excited to be doing something different again, but the closer we came to departing, the more I was tiring of the whole business.

Upon further reflection I considered how comfortable and disinterested I'd become, hidden away from the world in my luxury penthouse, surrounded by my many symbols of success and international acclaim. At this stage of my career, the thought of trekking through mosquito-infested wilderness and sleeping on the ground had no appeal. Then again—time away from the daily drudgery of deadlines and the constant squabble of tawdry office politics might be just what I needed to ignite a spark of ambition.

As the preparations drew to a conclusion, my participation was lukewarm at best. In fact, I'd almost decided this would be my last foray into the great unknown, that my time had come to wind down and prepare for early retirement. I'd managed to accumulate more money than I could ever spend, so what was the point of doing more?

But as we bounced around in terrible turbulence and challenged every law of aeronautical physics to remain airborne, my only hope was to live long enough to reach our destination. I can still recall the feeling that if we should survive to tell the tale, any story—no matter how earth-shattering—would be but a small bonus. Inside my head an irrepressible voice screamed in terror, "Oh God, if you're out there, please save my sorry soul!"

A sound from the cockpit interrupted my nightmare.

"Hey! Almost there," the pilot called as he wrestled with the controls. I glanced to the GPS and watched the numbers count down to the pre-set grid reference. Moments later the plane burst out of the narrow gorge into a deep valley. We peered below, intently scanning the scenery, but there was little to see through the late morning mist.

"We need to be lower!" I called over the angry roar of the engines. At my comment the pilot leaned on the stick, and I grasped the under-frame of my seat as we plummeted hundreds of feet in a few short seconds.

At the bottom of our rapid descent, I gathered my composure as best I could and looked out to survey the surroundings. Through the haze we could now make out the square boxes we'd come so far to see.

In quiet excitement I yelled to the pilot and pointed to my camera. He understood my intention and eased back on the throttle to slow our approach. We snapped a few shots on the first pass, but we were still too high to see clearly.

Gesturing again, I traced circles in the frosty air. The plane banked gracefully as we flipped around for a second pass. This time I could make out small rectangles within the larger squares, giving the appearance of buildings connected by roads or waterways. Crops were also visible, indicating habitation and recent activity.

The plane was quite low for the final run. Our cameras clicked and whirred as we flew over several walled cities of considerable size. I could now see people and animals scurrying to and fro like tiny insects. As I looked around the cabin to the members of my team, an air of excitement came over us.

"Looks like we have something to write home about after all!" I jested.

The plane set down in the deep valley not far from one of the walled cities. Climbing from the confines of that flying tin-can brought so much relief to my pounding heart that even if we'd found ourselves in the depths of hell, I would have been thankful. But this place was nothing like the hellish barren waste I'd expected. As I beheld the vast expanse, my first impression told me we had landed in nature's paradise.

The floor of the valley was below the snow line, where the earth was alive with tiny wild-flowers. My eyes beheld their bright colours like bold blotches on an artist's palette. Surely there was never a runway so beautiful in all the world.

Amid the magnificent spendour, I noticed a group of natives gathered along the tree-line not far from the plane. They appeared inquisitive but not aggressive. There was no sign of weapons or any hint of hostility, though our nervous navigator held tight to his rifle as we unloaded my gear.

Frenzied thoughts flashed through my head as I faced my moment of truth. We had buzzed several of their square cities and documented as much as we could from the air. It was time to get closer and find out more, something I'd always preferred to do alone. This could prove to be a dangerous exercise, yet I felt no cause for alarm. After all, what could there be to fear in a paradise such as this?

Making contact was always the most crucial part. If I got it wrong, there would be no story and no considerable pay-cheque. Undaunted, I shouldered my heavy pack and checked the pistol strapped to my belt. I was uncertain about carrying a firearm, but we reasoned that doing so could mean the difference between life and death, so I buckled up and flicked open the clip for quick access.

All was set. I exchanged parting nods and a few last words before swallowing hard and heading off toward the gathering crowd. I remember that walk with absolute clarity. They were the first steps of a remarkable journey—a journey destined to change the course of my life beyond all recognition.

As I approached the group of natives, a small aged man came forward with hands held wide.

"Welcome!" came the warm greeting in a loud, distinctive voice. "I am Mahonri, son of Melesch and Tepa. Welcome to Yuwmah!"

"You speak English?" I gasped.

"I speak many languages, my young friend," came his smiling reply.

I quickly established that I could accompany them to their city. Without formality we set off, as though nothing further needed to be said, and walked in silence across the pristine landscape.

As we made our way through the lush forest, I took mental notes, a skill honed over several decades. The people were friendly and not perturbed by a pale-faced visitor dressed in strange clothes who had descended from the sky in a giant silver bird. Perhaps they were aware of aeroplanes and people from the outside world, but I thought it unlikely.

The older members of our party, though quite short, appeared strong and athletic. Even the elderly among them were surprisingly sprightly, and it was difficult to guess their age. They showed no sign of infirmity, unlike most of our senior citizens back home.

I marvelled at the simplicity of their clothing. Both men and women wore similar attire. A light collared robe fell to just above the knee over loose-fitting trousers to the ankles. A few wore a heavier poncho against the chill of the mountain breeze. Around their necks hung elaborate beads and brightly coloured scarves. Several of the men wore three-sided hats and scant beards. Their elegant yet simple attire and prim presentation gave the impression they had dressed to welcome a famous visitor. Of course, I was not famous and my arrival was not anticipated. Or was it?

My preoccupation with my escorts was broken as we emerged from the trees to stand at the edge of a beautiful vista. In the foreground were golden fields of wheat and a vast expanse of a bushy plant I later learned was quinoa. To one side was a patch of corn, and to the other a flock of sheep grazed lazily on stubble.

Past the fields was a massive stone wall, perhaps twenty feet high, stretching a mile or more from east to west. The enormous stones stacked tightly together formed a vast fortress, towering above us as we approached.

My welcoming party proceeded across the fields on a baked earthen road as hard as concrete from hundreds of years of traffic. The noisy clomping of my hard soled boots embarrassed me. My companions' moccasins were silent. No one appeared to notice my plodding, but I felt uncomfortable. The intrusive noise seemed grossly out of place in this peaceful paradise.

At the imposing entrance, the sound of a giant bell tolled—three deep bursts of three sharp rings. I wondered what the signal meant. Our party entered the walled city through an arched gateway beneath a large plaque adorned with elaborate pictorial characters. Huge timber doors swung on massive hinges at either end of the short tunnel. Walking close together into the semi-darkness, we hurried through the narrow passage to the brilliant light beyond.

Emerging from the tunnel, I was so distracted that I struggled to keep up. More overwhelming than the scenery was the feeling in the air. There was an energy here: an invisible essence that permeated every pore like a warm breeze. I felt changed—my body enlivened and my spirit quickened.

Against the inside of the wall was a row of low dwellings stretching as far as the eye could see, each one sharing common walls with their neighbour. The fronts of the dwellings were made of brownish mud-brick. A heavy wooden door was set in the centre with narrow windows about five feet high on either side opening onto a low veranda. Each door was distinctly painted with an unusual array of earthy colours and symbols.

The dwellings had baked clay-shingled roofs with a long rectangular window set on each one. Most were open like a giant trapdoor to offer a cool breeze against the midday heat. As I observed their construction, I entertained the notion that sky windows would be ideal for the steamy suburbs back home. The thought crossed my mind that I could start a new trend and make some serious money from such a unique and practical idea.

Along the wide cobbled road, a series of stone buildings similar to those found in ancient Greece or Rome came into view. The structures were of grand design, with elaborate architecture, massive columns, and domed roofs. The gardens were immaculately kept. Sculptured statues and picturesque fountains stood amid vast manicured lawns. Decorative latticework covered in climbing roses and assorted creepers lined the paths to offer shade. A five-piece orchestra of unusual instruments played in the open area between the buildings. Their sweet music wafted through the trees like birdsong. The cultural ambience was most impressive.

Beside me, the elderly Mahonri was wearing the broadest of smiles.

"Does our city meet with your approval, Mr Saomes?" he enquired, reading the answer from my expansive gaze.

"It is certainly different," was all I could manage.

"Yes," he nodded. "Of course, the nature of any city is subject to its ethos and design. We could have many rows of houses within these great walls, with streets and walkways, and tens of thousands of inhabitants. But big cities do not make for the kind of peace and safety we desire. Instead, we choose to overlook the temptation to maximise economic measures and strive instead to create an environment where our happiness is the first and greatest consideration. So, we have minimal housing, which allows for more natural and peaceful surrounds where we dwell in complete comfort.

Happiness and the freedom to achieve it for ourselves are the heart of all we hold dear, Mr Saomes."

Further down the road, an expansive area opened before us. A large roofed structure without walls stood in the centre, ringed by hedges and gardens. Under the tiled roof were perhaps twenty men and women, sitting in silence on the far side of a massive stone table. As we drew closer, most of our group stopped short and sought the shade of the magnificent canopy of trees around the perimeter.

Mahonri leaned towards me and squeezed my arm just above my elbow. "I will be your spokesman," he said kindly. "I must introduce you to the council of elders. It is they who will approve your stay among us."

He'd gotten me this far in a potentially hostile environment, so I felt to follow his lead. I surveyed the circle of faces as they looked at me, their faces serious and contemplative.

"We see a stranger among us. Who speaks for this man?" came a sharp and penetrating voice in clear English. Mahonri ushered me forward, bowing politely.

"I, Mahonri will speak for this man," he said firmly.

"What is his purpose here, Honourable Mahonri?" came the questioning reply.

Mahonri turned and asked in solemn tones, "How shall I answer?"

Stepping forward in what I thought was a brave gesture, I boldly asked, "May I speak for myself?"

"Who are you that we might listen?" came the retort.

11

Somewhat stunned I answered as forthrightly as I could. "My name is John Saomes of Brisbane, Australia, a country far away."

"We are well aware of where Brisbane is located, Mr Saomes. What is your purpose here?"

"Your city is visible to our satellite in the sky above, and I have come to investigate."

"And what shall you do with such information should we allow you to gather it, Mr Saomes?" came the voice after a brief pause.

"We plan to publish our findings in a magazine for the entire world to read."

"And do you seek our permission, Mr Saomes, or only our compliance?"

I was dumbfounded. These were cultured people of considerable civility, and not the primitive savages we expected. My unease must have shown because the voice at the centre of the table spoke again before I could reply.

"We do not mean to unsettle you, Mr Saomes, but we are concerned at your intentions. As a peaceable people, we are reluctant to allow anything to transpire that may threaten our sheltered existence."

"I understand," I said, hoping they would believe me. "I do not wish to cause you or your people any harm."

"Then perhaps you would secure your firearm, Mr Saomes. Your holster is open and your hand is at the ready to draw."

Again I was amazed. They knew of guns, yet I saw no sign of weapons among them. They had knowingly allowed me to walk into their midst with my sidearm poised for action, yet they took no apparent measures to protect or defend themselves.

At that moment I felt out of my depth and extremely uneasy. As I moved my hand toward the open holster, the urge rose within me to draw the weapon for my own protection. I shivered like a trapped animal surrounded by a pack of ravenous dogs. Mahonri sensed my insecurity, and in one smooth motion he stepped to my side and reached his hand to secure the heavy clip.

"May I speak for you?" he asked with a hint of desperation.

"Yes, of course!" I stammered.

"Honourable Elders, Mr Saomes has travelled a great distance to investigate and document our civilisation. He has shown much determination and courage in coming here and seeks only to understand our ways. Most of all he requests our hospitality and cooperation. He means no harm. His is a noble endeavour for which we may one day be grateful. Indeed, his exploits here may benefit the entire world."

"And what will he give us in return for our hospitality and cooperation, Honourable Mahonri?" returned the booming voice.

"I have gifts!" I blurted. "Beads, mirrors, and precious things for you and your people." Opening my pack I took out the bag of plastic treasures my editor's secretary had chosen for just such an occasion.

I placed them on the stone table, stepping back to rejoin Mahonri who had become my only source of protection.

The Chief Counsellor shot me a glance of apparent disdain. There was murmuring among the others around the table as they examined a few objects and cast them aside in disgust.

"I see nothing of value here, Mr Saomes. These are cheap trinkets to appease the inquisitiveness of a backward and primitive civilisation. Let me assure you, we are neither primitive nor backward here. We have no need of such 'baubles and beads'."

Again Mahonri spoke to rescue me.

"Chief Councillor, what would you esteem to be of value that Mr Saomes may bestow upon us in return for our hospitality and cooperation?"

I felt empty. What could I possibly give these people? I thought of my pistol and reached for the buckle, but Mahonri stayed my arm and gave it a gentle squeeze. I froze and stood in silence, waiting for what seemed an eternity for the response.

The Chief Councillor was now looking directly into my eyes with incredible intensity. His stare pierced my being like a lance of invisible light. I felt the depths of my soul being probed and weighed. It was not a pleasant feeling, but I held his stare, allowing him to evaluate me with his penetrating gaze.

Finally, he spoke. "I sense you are an honourable man, Mr Saomes, but we are an ancient people with much to protect. We are aware of the current circumstances among the nations, and the perilous directions many have chosen to follow. There is much here in our city of Yuwmah that would be of benefit to the fledgeling world. I propose that we will share with you our ways, Mr Saomes, if you grant us one thing. The thing we ask of you is anonymity. We wish our location to remain anonymous. Our people would not welcome being inundated with scores of inquisitive visitors as a result of your article. We seek only to be left in peace."

I moved to speak but Mahonri squeezed my arm more forcefully and spoke again. "If Mr Saomes will give his word that he will maintain our anonymity, Chief Councillor, may he be permitted to live among us and learn our ways?"

The Chief Councillor looked to the men seated to his right and left. Each nodded in turn. Then came the echoing voice. "I propose that Mr Saomes may remain among us as long as he keeps our ways and walks in all manner of righteousness, and pledges that our anonymity will be respected and preserved. Will anyone challenge this decision?" he asked boldly, looking about for any sign of dissent.

Again I moved to speak, but before I could do so, Mahonri turned to me with upheld hands, "Will you give such an undertaking to the Council, Mr Saomes?"

"I will," came my firm reply.

"In the absence of a challenger—so shall it be," said the Chief Councillor. "Welcome to the city of Yuwmah, Mr Saomes. You are now among friends."

The men and women seated around the stone table stood in unison and walked toward me. Each one introduced themselves in perfect English and welcomed me with a hearty handshake. I felt deeply moved by the warmth of their words, their gentle smiles and kind gestures.

Within the space of an hour, my journey of discovery had taken an unforeseen turn. In my mind I saw myself arriving as the conquering hero, armed with higher education and superior technology. I had descended among primitive savages as a God adorned in fine clothes, only to be cut down like an insignificant sapling in a forest of giants. For all I had made of myself in forty years of life, among these people I felt almost childlike. Oh, how the mighty had fallen.

CHAPTER 2

The Yuwmahns were an indecipherable mix of ancient and modern, of primitive peasantry and learned world citizens.

A fter the pleasantries of my welcome, Mahonri escorted me back along the cobbled road with a glowing smile.

"You are relieved, Mr Saomes," he said with a sense of certainty.

"If only you could know how relieved," I replied. "Your people are not as I expected."

"There is much for you to learn from us my young friend. For now though, it is the time of rest and the passing of the heat of the day. We shall talk more this afternoon."

Mahonri led me to one of the mud-brick dwellings that would become my home for the duration of my stay, and bid me farewell. I entered cautiously to find myself in an 'L' shaped living room with two smaller rooms off to the side and rear. There were wooden seats around the ageless walls and a massive table with low stools in the centre. A stone fireplace was built into the back corner. Recessed into the central wall was a large urn beside a dark stone basin.

As I surveyed the room in silence, a gentle voice came from behind me. I turned to see a young man with a broad smile standing in the doorway.

"Welcome, Mr Saomes. I am Pahoran, your neighbour to the east." At my beckoning he gave a respectful bow of the head and entered.

"If you would allow me, I will help you," he said.

"Thank you, Pahoran," I replied, stepping back. Walking briskly to the urn, he began my tour.

"Water passes overhead each day and fills your jug to overflowing so you will always have plenty. The spillage drains into the sewer below. This basin is for washing the hands and face."

He moved to the first door. "This is the parents' retreat where you will sleep and store your things. There are clothes and shoes you may wish to wear for your comfort."

Moving to the second door, Pahoran opened it wide and pointed inside. "This is the private room where parents and children wash and dress."

The small room was barely eight feet square. Set into the floor was a dish-shaped stone tub.

"If you release this cord, the water falls from above

like rain," he continued, touching a long leather strap secured by a hook beside the door. "You may shower or bathe at your leisure," he added.

"In the corner is the toilet. It may appear crude by your standards, but it is very practical and functional." My eyes moved to the unusual looking throne. There were two wooden slats atop a low pedestal. A third removable slat encased in leather was wedged across the centre.

"The sewer below is flushed regularly," said Pahoran. "There is no need to do more than replace the lid after use."

There was no evidence from the outside of running water or a sewage system, so this was a level of technology I hadn't expected.

Next, Pahoran led me to a small cupboard in the corner against the front wall.

"In here is a plate of biscuits and a jug of fruit juice. You may eat as you desire. Cereal, bread, fruit, and milk, are available after sunrise in the city square. We assemble there for breakfast and the evening meal."

"Now is the time of rest. When the sun passes, I will return. If I can assist you, I will be next door," he said, pointing. "I bid you a peaceful afternoon, Mr Saomes." Without further comment he bowed his head, smiled, and departed.

Alone in my new abode, I surveyed the humble surroundings and was struck by their simple functionality. Parents could raise a large family here in relative comfort. All the essentials of civilised living were well established. As a dwelling, it was a secure sanctuary with a rustic, homely feel; far more than I had anticipated finding in these ancient surrounds.

I carried my pack into the parent's retreat, sat on the corner of the bed and kicked off my heavy boots. My mind was weary from the happenings of the morning. Today had been incredibly eventful. I lay back on the soft blanket and felt my tired frame relax into the comfortable mattress, eyes looking up at the sky through the window in the roof to watch the clouds floating effortlessly by.

I must have fallen into a deep sleep because on awakening I felt groggy and momentarily disorientated. My body came alive slowly, rejuvenated from the midday nap. As I took in the surroundings, I noticed three robes, several pairs of trousers, and shoes hanging on wooden pegs. There were ponchos too, and a funny three-sided hat. I took them down for closer examination.

The material of the light coloured robe and trousers was a rather heavy weave but silky to the touch. It had the appearance of a cotton and wool blend, but I was no expert. The heavier poncho was probably wool. It was intricately designed in beautiful patterns and earthy colours. The shoes looked like bedroom slippers but with long laces and thick soft soles.

To my surprise, everything fitted—probably because they were 'one size fits all' with ample adjustment. Even the shoes were made to fit a variety of sizes. Pulling the laces caused them to hug my feet snugly. I smiled to myself as I paraded around the room. There was no mirror so I could only imagine how I looked.

"If only my favourite secretary could see me now!" I said aloud.

The ancient dress was much to my liking so I decided to wear it. I felt free and unrestricted, and very light and casual. I was also more than a little hungry. In the living room, I poured water into the basin and dampened the small cloth to wipe my face and neck. The chunky bar of unscented soap made my hands feel clean and refreshed.

As I sat at the massive table, I realised I was feeling good in quite an unusual way. I had the impression of waking on a day when I didn't have to work or meet a deadline. Actually, it was more like being on holiday, a pleasure I hadn't experienced since I can't remember when. The feeling remained with me as I helped myself to the biscuits on the earthen plate. They were filling, although less appetising than my usual pastrami and salad sandwiches with a white tea and doughnut. Still, this far from home, what more could one ask for?

I opened a narrow window and looked out into the street. People were coming and going, with most heading towards the city centre. Everyone seemed happy and excited. I wondered why.

It was then that Pahoran came into view, still wearing that broadest of smiles. He beckoned me to join him with a gentle wave of his hand.

"Come, Mr Saomes," he said in a youthful voice. "We must go to the gathering place."

As we walked, Pahoran told me about himself—that he lived alone, that he would soon be married, and how excited he was to finally take his place among the grown-ups. I was impressed by his maturity as we talked about my journey, and 'what motivates a man to risk his life in pursuit of a story of strangers'.

"I have not yet been to the greater world," he said. "Our people are discouraged from travelling while we are young. Only those whose children are independent are advised to leave our city."

"You know of the greater world, Pahoran?" I asked.

"Oh yes," he replied. "Our people have been travelling there for centuries. I hear that in recent times their journeys have become exceedingly complex and dangerous. Several of our people have never returned, causing much concern and contemplation among our elders."

I couldn't help but wonder at his concept of 'the greater world'. Was it confined to a few days journey to neighbouring villages, or were these people really world travellers? I wondered how I might find out?

"So, where in the greater world would you like to visit, Pahoran?" I asked.

"Oh, there are many places," he replied. "I would like to visit the Greek ruins and the remnants of the great empire of Rome. I would also like to visit London, New York, and Hong Kong. Most of all though, I would like to visit your Great Barrier Reef and see the beauty of the tropical fish among the corals. I am told it is a sight to behold. Those who have been there say it is the most impressive of all the world's seven natural wonders."

His broad smile broke again as he drifted off in thought. His face told me he was far away on a tropical shore with the wind in his hair and salt on his lips.

We walked on through a sparsely treed area with immaculate lawns, flowing fountains and sculpted figures. The area reminded me of the set of a play I saw in high school. The surrounds were much like the backdrop of the scene where all the Gods had gathered in Heaven to discuss the future of those on earth.

"What are these buildings among the trees, Pahoran," I enquired.

"That one is the grain store," he said. "Over there is the building where wool and cotton are spun and woven into fabric. That one is where tools and other implements are kept, and this one is where things are made from wood. The mill is outside the city walls. Only dressed timber is brought here."

As we continued, Pahoran pointed out other buildings along the way.

"Over there in the distance is the library where the records of our ancestors are kept. All the books acquired from around the world are housed there. And this building is ... It is hard for me to translate!" he exclaimed. "It is a repository of things brought back from the greater world over the centuries. I am not yet old enough to enter there, but Master Mahonri may show you if you would like."

"I most certainly would like," I replied. "As for your translation, your English is excellent, especially for one so young."

"I thank you, Mr Saomes," he answered. "As children we learn English, French, German, and Spanish, as well as our mother tongue. It is the Adamic language: the language which Adam and Eve spoke in the Garden of Eden, the language that God speaks in Heaven," he said confidently. "Once we learn to speak the language of Adam, all other languages are much easier to understand, although you may think we speak them awkwardly. Many of our elders also speak Hebrew and Mandarin, and of course Greek and Latin. I have much yet to learn, Mr Saomes."

I sat subdued as I contemplated the scope of the Yuwmahn culture. They had travelled the world for centuries. Therefore, they had knowledge of technology far beyond anything I'd seen here. My mind filled with questions. Why did they remain in such a primitive state when they could so easily improve their situation? Why did they choose to dwell in this wilderness when they had the wherewithal to live elsewhere?

The Yuwmahns were an indecipherable mix of ancient and modern, of primitive peasantry and learned world citizens. These inconsistencies puzzled me. Was their system of government really as revolutionary as they claimed? What was it about their way of life that kept them living as they did? These and other questions haunted me and I struggled to make sense of them.

CHAPTER 3

Finding happiness is the object and design of our existence,
and will be the end thereof if we pursue the path
that leads to it.

O n reaching the city centre, I saw Mahonri seated at one of the stone tables with several men his own age. I could hear them laughing loudly as if someone had made a joke. It was indeed a heart-warming sight.

"Ah, Mr Saomes, and Pahoran," Mahonri called as we approached. Almost in unison the men moved to accommodate us around their table. "Tequill has been entertaining us with a story of his trip to Paris," Mahonri began. "A group of children mistook him for Toulouse Lautrec!" At his remark they burst into laughter again, and I found myself laughing with them.

"I've always wanted to travel to Paris but I've never had the chance," I said.

"You are young, Mr Saomes. Your opportunity may one day come to you. I can highly recommend it as a place of tremendous interest," said Mahonri.

"Especially the Left Bank!" exclaimed Tequill. They burst into laughter anew, savouring the remnant of the joke I'd missed.

The stone tables were set beneath magnificent trees offering shade and shelter like the canopy of a huge tent. Small birds chattered in the branches above while larger birds with brightly coloured plumage paraded around the lawns. In many ways it was a modern setting where people could sit in large numbers and pass the afternoon in pleasant conversation.

Hundreds of people were milling about in small groups. They sat at tables and on long stone benches. Some crouched or reclined in circles on the lawn while others leaned against trees in twos and threes. As we chatted, the question of why everyone had assembled continued to elude me.

"So gentlemen, what is our purpose here?" I asked, directing my query to no one in particular.

"Do you mean 'here' as in 'here upon the earth', Mr Saomes, or are you only referring to our gathering this afternoon?" Mahonri replied light-heartedly.

"Both are good questions Mahonri, but my immediate concern is with the lesser question," I answered.

"Oh well, I hope you are not too disappointed, Mr Saomes, but we have gathered here this afternoon to discuss the greater question," he answered with a smile.

My mouth fell open in awe. Unless my ears deceived me, the inhabitants of this remote and uncharted village had come together to consider the meaning and purpose of life. I sat in stunned silence, waiting for the discussion to unfold.

"Here in Yuwmah, we meet regularly to discuss the principles of our existence and how they might relate to the many aspects of our civilisation, Mr Saomes. To the Yuwmahn mind, the philosophical aspects of life are among the most fundamental of all areas of learning."

"Of course, we are well aware that such conversations are rare in the outside world, and generally left to the academics. But here in Yuwmah, we deem such understanding as an essential component of the very fabric of our civilisation and the foundation of all we say and do. As a people we are not concerned with having to work every day or with the acquisition of money, so we aren't consumed with such distractions as most are in the capitalist world. As a society we are not enslaved by the system that governs us. We are free to think and ponder, and to exercise our minds towards every aspect of our happiness and advancement."

Mahonri continued, "We gather often to discuss and postulate ideas—to better understand life's deeper meanings, and to clearly identify the path that leads to the pinnacle of our existence. We propose to maximise our potential and prosper every manifestation of that which we consider beneficial and good. In short, we hope to find a more excellent way. We strive to be the best we can, to enjoy the greatest happiness this life might offer us. Does our purpose here this afternoon appeal to you, Mr Saomes? Does it arouse your interest?"

"Oh yes!" I replied. "I think it's quite incredible! And might I add that if those watching from afar were wondering what was being discussed, I feel sure they would never guess!" I laughed.

"Quite so," Mahonri continued with a brief smile. "So, may I enquire, Mr Saomes—what say you to how we came to be? What meaning do you attribute to your existence, and what do you propose is our greatest purpose? Have you thoughts or beliefs you might like to share?" came the gentle request for my participation. Once again I found myself out of my depth, though I was sure I was about to learn something of tremendous value if I could only keep up with the conversation.

"To be honest, these are not questions I've considered to the point of finding answers," I admitted. There are numerous fables and theories around the world. Many believe the evolutionary process best explains our existence, while others suggest that we came from outer space. In the west, both theories are acceptable, but no one really knows for sure. Do you have answers to these questions, gentlemen?"

Young Pahoran appeared to feel the need to show his metal in front of his elders. He looked to the older men who shot him encouraging glances. Leaning forward, he began to speak with authority, to postulate the beliefs of his people.

"We believe that mankind is a dual being, Mr Saomes. Our physical body was created for us by earthly parents from the dust of the earth. Our spirit gives the body life. The spirit is the same shape as the physical body, but our spirits are the literal offspring of heavenly parents. Our spirit descended from the heavens at the time of our mortal birth. We were created in the image of our heavenly parents, Mr Saomes, both male and female. Having life means we have the divine right to choose for ourselves the kind of life we desire most."

"Our greatest purpose here is to find the greatest happiness, which means we must learn the most important lessons of life—most of all to think and act for our own betterment. In learning to act for ourselves, we also learn to act for the betterment of all, because our personal happiness depends on others being happy too. As we learn these lessons, we become more like those who created us—perhaps even to qualify ourselves to return to our heavenly home to become as our heavenly parents for all eternity."

Pahoran then looked around the table as if to glean feedback of how well he was doing. The older men smiled and nodded their approval.

"What say you to our beliefs, Mr Saomes?" asked Mahonri in a quizzical tone.

I knew I would have to be careful here, but I thought there was no harm in a few questions.

"Indeed an intriguing proposal, and one I am somewhat familiar with. An interesting take on the creation story, a belief held by many religious communities around the world. May I inquire as to the basis of your doctrine?" I asked to no one in particular.

Again Pahoran leaned forward. "We know this to be so, Mr Saomes, because the Divine One visited and lived among us. He taught us from his own mouth. From Him we learned the language of Adam, which is a perfect language. We also learned how to live at the pinnacle of our potential, to understand the way to establish the best possible society. The 'divine way' has stood the test of time, and kept us free from the problems of the modern world."

"The Divine One taught us many things, Mr Saomes. Most of all, the things of life that matter most, of richness and beauty, and joy without end. He turned us from warring and hostile animals to a peaceful and noble people who no longer make war, who genuinely care for each other. Then he returned from whence he came and left us to learn for ourselves."

"So, how do you interpret the greatest purpose of life, gentlemen? How do you strive to become like your God?" I asked.

"This may appear to be a complex question, Mr Saomes," replied Pahoran, "but the answer is not. That is to say, the answer is simple, but living the way to achieve it is not so straightforward. The Divine

One taught us that the purpose of this life is to learn to choose right from wrong—that by our righteous choices we might find the greatest happiness of all."

"In his own words, 'Finding happiness is the object and design of our existence, and will be the end thereof if we pursue the path that leads to it.' This is the answer to our highest purpose," added Pahoran.

"But there is more, Mr Saomes," Mahonri continued, "and this is perhaps the most exciting part. In finding true happiness, we also find other aspects of Godliness, even to understand the principles of Heaven. As for the meaning of life, which is a very different but related concept, I would propose an answer that is equally simple. Having life and being alive means we can choose for ourselves how we live. We can choose to act for ourselves rather than merely being acted upon by the world around us. To the Yuwmahn mind, the right to choose our own destiny is the most fundamental of all."

"So, life is a journey from birth to death, Mr Saomes. The purpose of life is not to merely survive to the end. The end will come in its own good time. The purpose of life is more about finding the path that leads to the better end—and learning to follow it."

"You see, life can be such a beautiful experience if there is joy in the journey. The quality of our life is measured by what happens along the way. When our purpose is to find joy in our journey, the end becomes almost irrelevant. So, day-by-day, our life unfolds and choices are placed before us. We find the greatest happiness when we learn to choose for ourselves the better way, which leads to the most favourable outcomes for all."

Pahoran broke in excitedly. "The happiness we seek is a lifelong happiness, Mr Saomes. We are not looking for simple fun. There is much fun to be had along the way, but the real purpose of our existence is to find the kind of happiness that is deep and lasting and eternal, that burns within us and fills us to overflowing."

Mahonri continued. "Ours is a simple walk, Mr Saomes. The object of our existence is to seek those things that will bring the greatest joy to all and eliminate every aspect that has the potential to rob us of the best this life might offer. So here in Yuwmah, our collective happiness is the central focus of our lives—the very heart of all we say and do."

"Planet Earth is not currently organised for the benefit of the people who live here," Mahonri added with a steely face. "In fact, in most situations, the happiness of the people is not considered. This is not as it should be and needs to be rectified if the world and its people are to find everlasting peace."

"By and large, the world is organised by a few faceless men for their own profit, and by governments who pursue secret agendas to support them. So in effect, most of the people are enslaved by a few self-serving masters who propose to control the entire population for their own advantage. Human happiness is not possible under such conditions. As a direct consequence, human misery is abundant everywhere. Even today, after the passing of thousands of years and many generations, vast numbers of people continue to live in poverty and squalor. Clearly this is not as it should be," he said again.

"But in Yuwmah, we have managed to eliminate human ambition for wealth and power. No one dominates anyone here, Mr Saomes. There are none who have authority over anyone else, except for family members raising children. Ours is a classless society where all may live in peace to follow the dictates of their own conscience and pursue their own desires— always for the benefit and betterment of all—not merely for ourselves."

"Our greatest achievement as a society is the ideal of losing ourselves in the service of others. No one works for themselves here. In Yuwmah, everyone is responsible for the happiness of all. No one profits from the ignorance of others or exploits those weaker or less capable than themselves. We have no kings or presidents who live in luxury at the expense of the workers. Indeed, we are all workers here. Each family must produce something for the collective table. This we do generously. So, as we give a little and receive much, in many ways we are also as kings and queens."

"And so, Mr Saomes, what we believe about the purpose and meaning of life is all important because it affects every aspect of our mortal journey. People who have no belief in any form of God are destined to live a lesser life because they have nothing to hold on to. This is the basis of the epidemic of spiritual poverty that is sweeping the earth as we speak. The humanists have done their best to destroy and remove any mention of God from the national conversation. The consequences of their meddling have seen many

I found myself nodding, but my nod was more than mere agreement. Through the course of our conversation I had reached a new depth of understanding. I had never regarded myself as a religious man, but I felt a certain conviction for their idea that the way we choose to live our lives matters—not only to ourselves but to others—and that collective happiness comes as a direct extension of our personal choosing.

CHAPTER 4

There are many things in the world that seem desirable,
but each has a consequence that is unacceptable to us:
a price we are not prepared to pay.

As we talked into the afternoon, a mother and son came to our table with a large basket of freshly washed carrots and several knives. Without a break in our conversation the men took the carrots and sliced them into pieces. I joined in the activity until the task was complete. Later, the mother and son returned and whisked away the basket with a grateful smile.

As our conversation continued, I gleaned as much as I could of the Yuwmahn beliefs.

"So tell me, gentlemen," I asked. "This 'best possible society' shown to your ancestors by the Divine One—have you maintained it to the present day?"

"Of course, Mr Saomes," came the stern reply.

Now I was confused. There was obviously much of worth here, but was this society the pinnacle of man's existence and truly representative of the best way for mankind to live and pass their mortal days? Was their community reflective of the way they believed God himself chose to live in the heavens?

"I see you are puzzled my young friend," exclaimed Mahonri. "Perhaps you are wondering if our civilisation is really as good today as one could ever hope for. Perhaps you see us as backward and primitive compared to your high-tech lifestyle in Australia. Is this your feeling?"

"Very much so," I replied. "You have so little in the way of technology. You don't have electricity. There are no machines, no computers, and few advancements of any kind that I can see. You don't have hot showers or cold drinks. How can this be the pinnacle of existence without such developments?"

I thought I'd argued a sound case and wasn't ready for the weight of the reply.

"We have no need of such things, Mr Saomes. Electricity and the associated contraptions it enables are fascinating and perhaps labour-saving, but quite unnecessary. In fact, they are often not beneficial for the body or the mind of man. If you light your fire, your shower will be warm, but hot showers and cold drinks are not good for the body or the belly, even though they may make us feel good. Have any of these so-called advancements brought you true happiness or a deeper sense of peace?"

"In the Yuwmahn world, our happiness is not dependent on technology. Neither do we seek immediate gratification or mere physical pleasures which fade like the setting sun. We seek to maximise our health and vitality, and promote the ultimate happiness for all—not to simply make life easier—for such was never the recipe for deeper happiness. Instead of relying on machines, we depend on the sun to rise each morning, the rains to fall and give life to our crops, the cycle of the seasons to give us balance and variety, and birth and death to fill the measure of our creation."

"We live in harmony with nature, Mr Saomes. We deplete none of the world's resources. All that we use is regenerated or recycled. We have no rubbish dumps! Neither do we have polluted air or water. There are no artificial additives or preservatives in our diet. Our food is fresh and nourishing. We are healthy and strong, and we suffer from none of the modern diseases of affluence. There are no heart attacks, cancers, asthma or high blood pressure, and no obesity or mental illness among our people."

"Many things in your world seem desirable, Mr Saomes, but each has a consequence that is unacceptable to us—a price we are not prepared to pay. So we reject them and refuse to embrace them because they are not to our ultimate benefit or advantage, even though they may seem desirable—even pleasurable."

"The electric light for example, illuminates the night like the noonday sun at the touch of a switch, but such is not good for our circadian rhythms and destroys the quality of our sleep. In Yuwmah, we rise with the sun and retire with it. Because of our strict observance to this natural cycle, our minds and bodies are invigorated and our senses are sharpened. Consequently, we are more aware of ourselves and more attuned and sensitive to the subtle inferences when communicating with others."

"It is written, Mr Saomes, that if we are to live long and be happy, we should eat less, and retire to our beds early. The soft light of a candle is not as destructive to the senses should we need to see in the dark. A good night's sleep is the most rejuvenating of all things and more beneficial than a healthy meal."

"We could purchase tractors and petrol to plough our fields; we could dig coal from the plains nearby to generate electricity for our city, and we could have all the things you have in the west. But to the Yuwmahn mind, the consequences are undesirable and often harmful. We find the ongoing social, emotional, and spiritual effects of mechanisation to be particularly stressful and destructive. Therefore, we reject such outcomes because they do not enhance the quality of our lives or add to our happiness."

"The bees give us wax for candles and honey for our table; the ox pulls our plough, pumps our water and crushes our grain. We are totally self-sufficient, Mr Saomes. We need nothing more to be happy than what nature provides."

"In our society, we have no unemployment. Even our young and elderly are gainfully engaged in purposeful and rewarding labours. Our work is performed on three days of our five day week—but never past midday. We do not live to work, Mr Saomes, and neither do we work just to live. We work only to provide for ourselves to satisfy our simple needs, for our health and learning, and the teaching of our youngsters. Consequently, we have no poor or needy, no beggars or slaves, no masters or bosses, and no politicians who make empty promises. Also, Mr Saomes, we have no police force, no prisons, and no crime or delinquency."

From what I'd seen during my few hours in Yuwmah, all they said was true, and I had to admit that a social structure as comprehensive as theirs was quite an achievement.

"Surely, there is an element of crime among your people," I pondered out loud.

"On occasions that is so," replied Pahoran. "I remember when I was a small boy, a man was found guilty of entering another man's home and stealing his neck beads."

"And what was his sentence?" I asked.

"He was cast out of the city to dwell in the wilderness, just like the murderer, the rapist, and the blasphemer; but I have never known such persons in my lifetime."

"But what of the concepts of repentance and forgiveness," I asked. "Can't he receive some form of punishment and eventually be forgiven of his wrongs?"

"Of course he can," replied Pahoran. Every man may choose to forgive others, no matter what has been done. But the criminal must endure the natural consequences of his actions. His punishment in the old days was to lose a finger. Even today, he may elect to receive such a punishment and remain among us. But if he steals again, he will be cast out, never to return."

"This may appear to be a harsh punishment for such a misdemeanour, Mr Saomes, but we have zero tolerance for crime here. When he chose to break our laws, he also chose the consequences of doing so. He knew the outcome of his actions before committing the crime—so in effect, he chose the associated punishment. Do you not see this as justice?" he asked firmly.

"I have to admit, it presents a compelling argument against becoming a criminal," I said thoughtfully. "So you don't believe in the death penalty?" I asked.

"Oh, yes we do, Mr Saomes. There are many heinous crimes that may be punishable by death. If there is no doubt of their guilt, then we slay the criminal element because the world is a better place without their kind. Why should anyone have to support such blights on society, to feed and watch over them while they waste away in a cell and contribute nothing? We find though, that being cast out usually brings the same end, eventually. The wilderness is a beautiful place to visit, but it is extremely harsh and cruel to anyone who is forced to dwell there alone."

"Have you ever had a prison system in your city?" I asked. They shook their heads.

"What purpose does it serve?" questioned Mahonri. "As with the western system, those who are punished most are the families of the criminals and especially their children. In many cases, criminals dwell in relative comfort and are dealt with so lightly that their punishment defies justice for their victims. Most of all, it entrenches their illegal behaviour and places an invisible label on them that is hard to shake off. Such a large proportion reoffend that it should be obvious to all that imprisonment is ineffective and a terrible waste of time and money."

"There is little reason to commit a crime in Yuwmah," said Mahonri. "All we need—our food, clothing, and accommodation are supplied at no cost by our honest labours. We have few personal possessions and there is no form of money. We simply have no need of it. So, there is no reason to commit a crime."

"No money!" I exclaimed. "Is there no form of exchange at all?" I asked.

"There is no exchange," said Pahoran. "Only in times of famine do we trade with the villages nearby, but that is extremely rare."

"Do you own personal property or goods which could be sold?" I enquired.

"None whatsoever," came the reply. "Everything we require is freely available to all. We have no need of ownership. All that is asked of us is to contribute our time and talents generously. There is a saying around the world that the hunger for money is the root of all evil. We believe this to be so in our society too."

"By eliminating money, Mr Saomes, we have taken away the major cause of class distinction. There are no rich or poor here. Everyone in Yuwmah is equal. But more than this, no one may covert the wealth of another or have the power to rule over them in their poverty. We have thus removed the prospect of anyone seeking domination or subversion. Our system is unsurpassed, Mr Saomes, ensuring a complete and all-encompassing way of life at the very pinnacle of human existence."

The entire community enjoyed a delicious meal together in the cool of the late afternoon. I was impressed by the order that everyone observed as they took their turn at the servery. There were no queue-jumpers, no pushing or shoving, and no undue mess, although several thousand people were amply fed.

In canteen style we helped ourselves to what was perhaps the most lavish and nutritious buffet I have ever seen. There were colourful fruits and salads, breads, unusual vegetables, and a variety of meat dishes I could not identify. There were condiments, gravies and sauces, all flavoured with herbs and spices to tantalise the most discerning pallet.

We drank water flavoured with fruit juice, or hot drinks like herbal teas. The food was prepared with considerable skill and tastefully presented to such a standard that even the most fastidious of connoisseurs would have been impressed.

I particularly enjoyed the light-hearted banter as we ate together.

"Do you like to read, Mr Saomes?" Mahonri asked. My blank face must have shown my disinterest because he continued without waiting for my answer. "Do you know that if you read a good book for just a few minutes each day, you can reach the equivalent of more than a dozen academic degrees in the course of your lifetime? To be a man of knowledge is to have the greatest power to choose. Knowledge is also the basis of all wisdom, an attribute we prize greatly."

"In our library we have books in many languages from all around the world. My personal favourites are the Iliad, the Odyssey, and the Margites, by Homer the Greek poet. Have you ever read these epics, Mr Saomes? I have read them to my children, my children's children, to their children and their grandchildren."

"Really! How old are you, Mahonri?" I asked bluntly in surprise.

"Time has little meaning to us here, Mr Saomes. There are those among us who count the seasons and the years, but I am not one of them. I do remember though, that I was married in the same year the world celebrated the dawn of a new century."

"You are over a hundred years old!" I blurted.

"Oh yes!" he exclaimed, "And my parents are even older! I must introduce you to them!" he laughed almost uncontrollably. It was the kind of humour everyone shared here. Indeed, they were a joyous people.

The meal continued for several hours as we chatted through the late afternoon. Afterwards I felt privileged to be included in a local ritual involving the most exquisite hot chocolate drink, with a strong flavour of hot chillies. I was told of the Yuwmahn dedication over thousands of years to develop the best cacao beans, and to master the science and artistry of making the most breath-taking chocolate drinks and confectionery. How strange this was, especially to one who was accustomed to eating in a noisy sports club or chewing through a tasteless TV dinner.

My team and I were of the opinion I had left civilisation behind in coming here, yet this meal and my time spent with the Yuwmahns in joyous conversation was one of the greatest examples of civility I'd ever witnessed. No one ate quickly. Every mouthful was savoured. Indeed, it was a grand feast, as elegant as anything I'd experienced anywhere in the world.

CHAPTER 5

*In our simplicity we have found peace. It is the perfectness
and peace the people of the world are desperately seeking,
which they cannot find in their complexity.*

Later that evening I lay on my bed watching the stars
as they sparkled down in all their magnificent glory,
though I scarcely noticed them. The conversations from
my first day in Yuwmah continued to confront me as if
I were reliving each and every moment. My mind was
awash with emotion as I made a few introductory notes
by the light of a large candle. Much had transpired that
I could barely comprehend, let alone write down in a
meaningful way.

The Yuwmahns claimed to have built a society that
represents the best way for mankind to live, yet they
regarded work as the very foundation of their existence.

Most people I knew would expect not to work at all in their ideal world. Did the Yuwmahn way truly represent the pinnacle of civilisation? I was not convinced, although I remained open to the possibility.

Yuwmahn life was markedly different from anything I'd ever imagined. I knew of populations whose existence revolved around procuring food: herders who moved their flocks up and down the mountains in search of grass, or fishermen who caught different varieties of fish from season to season. To those people, feeding themselves was the central focus of their community and their lives.

Other populations based their existence around trade, with caravans of camels, fleets of trucks or ships making long and arduous journeys as they carried their precious cargo to and from the great marketplaces of the world. In the west, financial considerations underlie virtually every decision, with economic viability as the primary determinant of western social structure. Nothing happens without weighing the cost or calculating the profit.

To Yuwmahns though, collective happiness is the first and most important measure of every decision. Yuwmahn lives revolve around their sources of joy: a few simple pleasures, security, achievement, freedom, and self-respect. Next to these aspects of their existence, almost nothing mattered. Yuwmahns are not consumed with agriculture, trade, or economics. Wealth and the pursuit of money are irrelevant. By their shared labours they are self-sufficient and completely content in their stress-free lifestyle. Little else is of any consequence.

I marvelled that they were an ancient culture who lived such uncomplicated lives. At times I was astounded by their excitement and the depth of their enjoyment of simple things. They laughed so freely and enjoyed every moment. Their love of life and nature and the natural ways was more inspiring than anything I'd ever witnessed.

Several comments from our discussions of the day bounced around in my brain demanding further consideration, but I hardly knew where to begin. My head spun with the volume of new information. Huge concepts required extensive processing before I could file them away. What a job! What an exhaustive task—and at the moment, what a mess!

"There are many appealing and pleasurable aspects of your world, Mr Saomes, but they have consequences we are not prepared to accept, a price we will not pay." This single statement deserved a lifetime of thought.

My notes continued: "We are an ancient people and highly evolved. Our society is stable. There is no need for change or ongoing reform. The only change in Yuwmah takes place in the hearts of the people, in the thoughts of our minds and the works of our hands, as we learn to govern ourselves more prudently for the greater benefit and happiness of all."

"Our needs are few. We want for nothing. In our simplicity we have found peace. It is the perfectness and peace the people of the world seek, which they cannot find in their complexity."

"The societies of the world desire to create perfect families, to live in a paradisiacal environment, and to enjoy a safe and peaceful existence; but they will never find such because of their complex and self-destructive lifestyle. Peace comes with sacrifice, Mr Saomes. The more you are prepared to do without, the simpler and less stressful life becomes and the greater your peace and happiness may be."

"Your fast paced life in the west requires too much effort just to get through the day. There is such pressure and tension, and so little real achievement. It is written that one should never confuse activity with accomplishment, Mr Saomes. In all of your activities day to day, what do you really accomplish?"

"And in your culture, a person's quality of life is almost completely governed by their job. One's role in society is very much a measure of who they are. Their income is the all-important determinant of the substance of their entire existence. Wealth is the limiting factor that predicates what they do, where they go, what they enjoy, and what they miss out on. When someone loses their job, their whole world collapses around them."

"In your social system, a few assume the role of masters while most are forced to be as slaves. But neither option is acceptable to us here. We have no masters and no slaves. We find the notion of subservience abhorrent."

"In Yuwmah, we help and support each other as equals. Many among us excel in a particular field of learning because of their personal efforts over and above the daily tasks that all perform. Of course, the added skills and abilities are of benefit to everyone, but someone who is skilled in the art of medicine and healing continues to work in the fields with the rest of us. Our collective participation in fundamental roles keeps everyone equal. Many of our people have developed specialised skills and knowledge, Mr Saomes, but we are not elevated above others as a result of them. Our additional skill set does not define who we are or reflect our personal worth."

"And once you choose a job or career in the developed world, you are required to pay rent or a mortgage to secure a place to live. This expense swallows up a large portion of your earnings, along with the many taxes you are also forced to pay. So, the government takes a huge chunk of your earnings as tax, and the bank or landlord takes most of the rest! Such a system holds no attraction to us here in Yuwmah, Mr Saomes. Most of your people are forced to work their life away in a never-ending struggle to merely survive!"

"In Yuwmahn society, all of our basic needs are catered for at no cost. As a result, our lives are spent pursuing interests that benefit ourselves, our families, and our whole community. 'Quality of life' and 'collective happiness' are the focus of our social system—not personal income or company profits."

"The best you can do in western society is to have more money than you could ever spend, but money alone is a poor reward. With money comes power, so you may own or possess anything you desire. However, possession and control are purely selfish ideals that offer little in the way of enduring happiness. Many become obsessed with ownership, but material possessions do not bring deep or lasting joy. The cycle of greed is such that we will always want more, and there will always be those who have more than you."

"We view consumerism as a pestilence," Mr Saomes. "Yuwmahns would sacrifice every possession in favour of personal enlightenment. If financial wealth is your treasure, you are destined to be poor forever. Neither wealth nor power bring true happiness. In Yuwmah we strive to reach the highest degree of personal fulfilment, which we share with others causing it to multiply manyfold. Life here is full of meaning and purpose of a more noble kind. Indeed, everyone is richer because we support each other. Is this not the better and more desirable way?"

I paused to consider my opinions. The Yuwmahns were extremely critical of the western world. I'd never considered our lifestyle to be decadent, and neither had I seen it as excessive or uncaring. Yet, upon reflection, there was plain truth in their words and substance to their arguments. I tried to weigh the strength of their comments, but there was too much information in my head to focus on a single issue.

"The world at large is poorly designed, Mr Saomes. Large cities create a sterile and unnatural environment that stifles the rhythms and cycles of the body and shrivels the spirit. Cities benefit the wheels of industry, but they do not benefit the people who live in them. There was a time when people lived in harmony with nature and the natural ways, in small villages and family groups where everyone supported each other. We need to return to that situation where life is about the happiness and advancement of all, where work is something we do to provide for ourselves and our family, and for the wealth and security of our community."

"Furthermore, we find the thought of supporting armies or a large contingent of public servants who produce nothing of tangible worth as sheer lunacy. And all the money spent on various programmes for people who have chosen not to provide for themselves and their own is unacceptable to the Yuwmahn mind."

"People must take responsibility for their own needs and put forth a little effort to help themselves, Mr Saomes. Our society has been organised so that everyone has the opportunity to do just that, in the simplest possible way. In Yuwmah we would never allow a segment of the population to make no worthwhile effort and live on welfare while others struggle or do without to sustain them."

"Everyone must strive to provide for their families, but that's all. Families must cover for those family members who do not contribute for a time. The contribution of

51

every family to the benefit of the greater community is the key to maintaining our freedom and our way of life. We do not spend our days working for a boss or a meagre portion of the profits. Quite the opposite. Through the course of our lives we aim to make everyone better off as a result of our efforts, including ourselves. We take immense pride in making a generous contribution."

"In Yuwmah we do not slave away month after month for a few weeks holiday. In our society we are almost permanently on holiday. Our city is like a giant vacation destination. To keep fit we work in the fields, not in gymnasiums. And most importantly, we all work together as equals."

"Outside of the few hours of labour, our lives are our own to do as we please. But if we want to eat and become recipients of all that is available to us, we must work to produce something so that our entire community is self-sufficient."

"We choose our labours and our area of endeavour, and strive to do our best for the sustenance and edification of all. Industry is the basis of our independence and freedom. It is the only mandatory aspect of our existence, although no one stands over us and keeps time. No one measures our efforts except God and ourselves. Virtually everything we do here, Mr Saomes, is very much up to us."

"Everyone has a role to play—from our youth, right through to the aged and frail. Our workday is about four hours, and only on three days of our five-day week.

Most of our time is spent on more meaningful pursuits. We value self-improvement and appreciate time with our family and friends. We encourage learning and the pursuit of excellence in all we say and do. We do not seek to be idle, Mr Saomes. We aim to improve and progress to a higher plane of understanding and achievement. Most of all, we seek to learn humility and charity, and to practice such in all their beauty and refinement."

"We choose to serve and support each other for our mutual benefit. We honour each other. We love and help each other. No one here is greater or lesser than any other, so there is no class distinction among us. We are all equal in a classless society, and the masters of our own destiny. No one owns or directs us. We are truly free!"

"The closest you come to real freedom in your world is to be financially secure—but that is not true freedom. Even when your home is your own and you have sufficient money for food, you continue to be compelled to obey a thousand rules and laws, supposedly for your protection. No one seems to approve of the endless regulations, yet you continue to allow the rules and the rulers to direct your life. We would never allow such a situation in Yuwmah!"

"We rest peacefully in our fortress. There is a level of security here that few experience anywhere in the world. You need not fear being harmed in Yuwmah,

Mr Saomes. Your only concern should be that you do not harm another."

"The Yuwmahn way involves no prisons, no crime, and few laws. Our system is complete and all-encompassing. Our way of life has not changed in hundreds of years. From generation to generation it remains constant, and so do we. There have been refinements over the centuries, most for only a short time, and the permanent changes are little more than fine tuning."

"Furthermore, we have no political unrest, or political parties who argue to control us. The established system we live by has served us well through many generations and has stood the test of time because it continues to uphold our freedom. We have no need of change, modernisation, or reform. We are completely content as we are."

My pen flashed from page to page as I recalled further comments and thoughts. I witnessed no one in Yuwmah who appeared unhappy or stressed. Everyone seemed content and at ease. There were no long faces or stern expressions. I saw no indication of frustration, jealousy, or resentment. No one yelled or spoke harshly. In fact, I hadn't heard anyone raise their voice.

As the night rolled on, I fell in and out of sleep. Often I found myself staring at the stars through the sky-window. Several times I rose from my bed and walked from room to room, struggling to come to terms with what I'd found here.

In the stillness before dawn I peered out through the narrow window at the empty street. In the western world there were always cars coming and going as people did what people do. But not here; everyone was at home. I returned to my bed. Sleep seemed impossible. I had to deal with the overwhelming turmoil in my head.

In the morning, I was to be given a grand tour of the city. Their words played on my mind. "Tomorrow you need not work, Mr Saomes, but you must choose an endeavour wherein you will play your part to contribute to the prosperity of our community." I felt as though I was back in school, choosing my future area of employment. I wondered at the career options. There were probably no openings for nuclear physicists or brain surgeons. Or were there?

CHAPTER 6

The elderly are honoured and highly esteemed. They are the most learned and knowledgeable, the wisest and gentlest, and the most capable teachers.

Morning came early, ushered in by the sound of heavy knocking on my front window. I woke from an incredible dream, only to find I was still pondering the events of the previous day. I sat up and slowly came to my senses, eventually opening the door to see Mahonri beaming with excitement.

"Good morning, Mr Saomes!" he greeted me with hands held wide. "Have you an appetite for breakfast?" After the feast we'd consumed the night before, I was surprised to find that I did. The thought of a repeat of last night's festivities made me all the more hungry. As we walked toward the city centre, I noted groups of people moving with purpose in all directions. Two and four-wheeled wagons drawn by horses and oxen rolled to and fro along the cobblestone road.

"A hive of activity this morning," I commented. "Is today of special significance?"

"Every day here is of special significance, Mr Saomes. Today is a workday, or at least the first half of it," came the reply.

We arrived at the servery and took bowls from the pile. The queue was short and moved quickly. I chose cereal from baskets, wheat biscuits not unlike muesli bars, cornbread, goats' milk, fruit, and juices. As a breakfast it was filling and substantial. We sat at the stone tables and ate heartily.

Pahoran soon joined us with a tall man named Kish who was introduced as the chairman of the coordinating council for farming and grazing. I thought Kish to be an important city official, but he quickly corrected me.

"I hold no authority or importance, Mr Saomes. Everyone works here to produce something. At the end of each season we hold a meeting to take stock of the harvest and to organise the proceedings for the following season. Our planning helps to produce the right food in the correct quantities. I have been elected as chairman of those meetings; that's all."

As we ate together Kish explained how every aspect of life in the city of Yuwmah was organised by the Yuwmahns themselves for their collective benefit. The usual practice was to form a committee, headed by an elected coordinator and aided by a first and second assistant.

"No one nominates themselves and there is no electioneering. If the nominee accepts the nomination, their name is placed over a barrel. If others think a particular nominee is the right person for the job, they vote accordingly by placing stones in the appropriate barrel." Kish explained.

"These are positions of responsibility rather than positions of authority, Mr Saomes," Mahonri interjected. "No one has any authority among us. The nearest we come to authority is the Grand Council before whom you appeared on your arrival. The Grand Council meets once a year, or as necessary, to consider changes or refinements to the laws of the city. They have no authority to change the laws, only to draft proposals at the behest of the residents. Their main role is to hear the petitions of the people, although for hundreds of years, life in Yuwmah has passed with little or no contention."

"Anyone may represent themselves before the council to have their petition recorded or have their idea added to the list of proposals for consideration. Each proposal is written on a noticeboard, which is placed over a barrel. To cast one's vote, you place a stone in the barrel, as with the election of officers."

"You may cast only one stone in any one barrel, but you may vote for several options if you find favour with more than one proposal, or simply refrain from voting if you have no preference or interest. In this manner, the most popular options are determined in true democratic fashion."

"So as you see, Mr Saomes, no one has any authority here. The process is set and simple to follow. It is also easy to administer. The outcome is always the expressed will of the community."

"How often do laws change?" I asked.

"There has never been a change in my lifetime or that of my father or his father." replied Mahonri.

"I believe the last contested issue was resolved by a single vote, cast by the most elderly member of our community in favour of carriages keeping to the right rather than the left," added Kish. "Out of respect, no one voted against her, and therefore no one needed to vote with her. As coordinator, I am required to sit on the Grand Council, but we have never had any such business placed before us, except for your arrival, Mr Saomes. In that case though, the precedents were set long ago. Our society is very stable. There is no need for change."

We finished our breakfast and rinsed our plates and cups in the tubs provided. Mahonri then grasped my arm. "I have a duty to attend to this morning that awaits me. I am to teach my great-great-grandchildren about the wars of our people. A history lesson, Mr Saomes! If you are interested, I will give you a summary this afternoon. For now though, Kish will escort you around our city. As you come to know the workings of the many parts, you may better understand the role and purpose of our activities here. I bid you farewell," he said, walking away with a polite bow of his noble head and an enormous smile.

Kish beckoned me in the opposite direction, and Pahoran followed a short step behind my shoulder. We walked to a large building near the eating area. Inside was the kitchen, with two long rows of tables down the centre and cooking facilities to either side. There were large bins along the walls containing baskets laden with fresh produce.

"As the harvest comes in from the fields, the baskets are passed through the appropriate window into the storage bins. From the bins, the produce moves to the central tables for preparation and then to the cooking and serving areas."

"And what of the waste?" I asked.

"There is no waste, Mr Saomes. What is not suitable for human consumption is passed on to the animals. We waste nothing here! Nothing at all!"

Assembled in the giant kitchen were groups of workers preparing vegetables for the evening meal. Some sang, others chatted, while others laughed and joked together. All were obviously happy, and no one appeared to object to their working conditions or the lack of wages.

"Hmm. There is certainly no sign of industrial action brewing here!" I thought out loud. Kish smiled.

"We have an old saying, Mr Saomes. He who strikes will be struck!" He chuckled heartily to himself as we moved on.

A short walk away was a smaller building where meat was stored and prepared. Kish explained that the slaughtering facilities were outside the main city wall. We would visit there later. We passed several long buildings set amid the spacious parklands on our way to the south gate. Kish explained the purpose and function of each as we walked.

Climbing the stairs beside the gate we passed two young men keeping a lookout over the fields beyond.

"What are they watching for?" I asked.

"They watch over the crops and animals, and will sound the bell if thieves should come upon us. They also watch for enemies and strangers," he replied, pointing to the large bell suspended over the stairway, "and they also look for the return of the Divine One."

"Watchmen are set at each gate twenty-four hours a day, Mr Saomes. The young men take their responsibilities quite seriously, and their regimented organisation serves as a marvellous preparation and learning for later years."

"Every individual who enters our city must be identified. Escorts are summoned and strangers must remain with their escort once they enter. Generally, the only acceptable reason to allow outsiders entry is to visit friends and family. Every two hours we rotate one of the watchmen. Each of our young men does a four-hour shift. Many things here are done in pairs, Mr Saomes. In this manner, there is one to teach and one to learn."

Pahoran spoke up for the first time, "This explains my accompanying you today, Mr Saomes. I am here as your escort, but also to learn and serve as I am instructed. I hope you do not mind my presence?"

Formulating my reply, I raised my hand to his shoulder and squeezed it firmly. "Your presence is comforting, Pahoran! I am pleased you are with us." This brought the broadest of grins to his young face. At that moment, I felt a hand in the middle of my back from Kish as if to quietly communicate a 'well said'.

As we walked onward, I considered the touch from Kish. The Yuwmahns cared for each other deeply and were acutely attuned to each other's feelings. This interpersonal sensitivity was a foreign concept in my world, yet I found it incredibly praiseworthy.

From the lookout we mounted a walkway that took us up the inside of the battlements. Kish's commentary painted a tense picture of hundreds of archers set along the wall with bows drawn, showering their arrows upon the approaching armies.

"We have fought such wars, Mr Saomes, but our city has never been taken. The fields are fertilised with the blood of our enemies," he said, pointing to the crops that flourished all around us.

Throughout the afternoon, I observed generations of men and women, who picked, weeded, and planted the fields of green and gold. It was a highly organised effort, yet no one appeared to be in charge.

Turning the corner, we headed north. A variety of vegetables came into view. There were cabbages, lettuce, and perhaps broccoli, and several other leafy greens I did not recognise. Perfectly parallel rows covered the terraces to the river beyond.

We paused on the wall at a patch of beans. Kish greeted the pickers in his own language. With much laughter and cajoling they threw a small bag of their produce up to Pahoran, who caught it smoothly and passed it immediately to Kish. The beans were delicious although not the stringless variety I knew from home.

As we walked and nibbled on the beans, we passed wagons heading into the city, loaded with food for the evening meal. Returning wagons brought tools, baskets, water, and fruit for the workers. Everyone seemed involved and contributed with enthusiasm. It was an impressive sight and an even more impressive ideal. I marvelled that such industry had continued for several millennia, solely by the collective efforts and agreement of the people.

Around the next bend were acres of fruit trees and vines planted in unusual patterns. The variety of colours made a beautiful mosaic upon the landscape. Flocks of sheep and goats grazed lazily under the trees, and hundreds of chickens and ducks scratched around a large pond beside the north gate. There were no fences or enclosures, except for the trellised grapes that acted as a natural barrier for protection and confinement.

At one point we came upon a father and three sons, tending a flock of sheep. At first I couldn't make out what they were doing, but Kish stopped beside me to watch the spectacle with considerable interest. It soon became apparent that the boys were trying to isolate and grab a particular sheep, but they were not fast enough to make the catch.

"Why doesn't the father step in to help the boys and spare the poor animal?" I asked in a puzzled tone.

"There is much to understand here, Mr Saomes," came the almost whispered reply. "This man is more concerned with raising sons than raising sheep."

As we watched in silence, I contemplated the importance of his reply. When the boys finally snared the elusive beast and toppled it to the ground, I felt a lump in my throat. The father ran in and hugged each boy. They were elated with their efforts. By the look of satisfaction on their faces, they had just won a gold medal at the Olympics. It was a very touching sight, even for a middle-aged man with no children of his own, and one I'll remember for the rest of my days.

Kish reflected on the incident as we moved onward. "Family is all-important here, Mr Saomes. The teaching of our young by those older and wiser is a major priority because it is crucial to their development. In Yuwmah we believe that spending quality time with our children is one of the most important things we can do."

"It must be a sad situation to wake each morning and go off to work all day to do something you have no passion for," Kish mused almost to himself. "We are greatly blessed here because our work ensures the survival and betterment of our community, but most of our time is spent on the aspects of life that are of greatest importance—on the things that really matter."

The next corner brought us to what appeared to be a small village outside the main wall. In the distance a placid river wound peacefully by. It was not a large river, but Kish commented that it provided a steady flow of clear water all year round.

"This is our industrial area," said Kish. "Any industries that have noise or an unpleasant smell are located out here. Because of the river, they are easily defended. Most of all though, they do not affect the beauty or tranquillity of the city beyond."

We descended the steps from the wall at the west gate and walked down the gentle slope to the river's edge. High on the bank was a series of stone tanks set into the main wall. Oxen were yoked and waiting nearby, harnessed to a giant water wheel.

"This is our pumping station," explained Kish. "Further down is another that pumps water directly from the river into the sewer system. This particular station is for drinking water." The water entered an ingenious filtration system using charcoal and sand. Kish explained how this was the highest point. From here the filtered water ran around the whole city several times each day. Because the waterways were open, they dried out between pumping times. This stopped the growth of algae and mosses that would clog the waterways if they were continuously filled.

We also saw the slaughterhouse, the extensive blacksmith's shop including a small smelter, the tannery, the apiary, the candle maker's hut, the pottery kiln, and a large grain mill.

As we concluded our tour, a wagon stacked high with bags of freshly milled flour was leaving for the storage shed in the city centre. At Kish's suggestion we climbed aboard and added ourselves to the load. The massive wheels of the wagon bumped over the cobblestone road as we trundled through the gate.

"It is almost the time of rest and the passing of the midday sun," said Kish. "Our tour will soon be over. Have you been impressed by our humble industry?" he enquired.

"I have indeed," I replied.

"Inside the wall is also a hive of activity, Mr Saomes. These buildings to the right are where our clothing is sewn. Wagon wheels are greased with fat and repaired in this shed. Baskets are woven and stored in that one, and shoes are made over there."

"Might I ask what role the elderly play," I enquired. "The elderly are honoured and highly esteemed," he replied. "They are the teachers of our children. While the parents are working in the fields for a few hours, the elderly take care of their grandchildren and great-grandchildren and so forth. They teach them the ways of our people and the languages of the world. They also teach them of science and mathematics, history and engineering, and war. Our education process is not about attending classes as it is in the outside world. We have not institutionalised education here. Wise family members teach the young when they feel they are ready. It is a far more personalised approach to education, not a forced exercise, and neither is it excessively academic."

"Most of all, the elderly teach the children to be humble, honourable, and compassionate. Charity, Mr Saomes, is among the greatest of all human attributes. Our older citizens are the most learned and knowledgeable, and the wisest, gentlest, and most capable teachers."

"Furthermore, their role is the source of much joy to them. They have the opportunity to pass on to their progeny the sum of their life's achievements. Anyone can pick corn, Mr Saomes, but teaching our children is the noblest of all honourable pursuits."

"So as you can see, the elderly are revered in our community. They are our greatest asset and our most precious resource. To be disrespectful to one's elders, and especially to our women, is one of the most serious crimes Pahoran or myself could ever commit."

Pahoran gave a small nod. "I am young and inexperienced, Mr Saomes. Of this I know. It is rare for a son to measure with his father at anything. But even more, it is unthinkable that I should dare to suggest that I know better than those who have gone before me. I have learned to revere those who have experienced so much and gathered knowledge and wisdom beyond my own. I have such respect for the sacrifices made by mothers, fathers, and the older generations that allow me to have the quality of life I now enjoy. I feel tremendously indebted to them for all that I have and all that I am becoming."

Pahoran hesitated for a thoughtful moment then added, "We are encouraged to choose for ourselves from a young age, Mr Saomes, but we are also encouraged to seek counsel from our elders before we act on our choices. Such is the strength of family."

Kish chimed in, "So you see, Mr Saomes, the exuberance of youth is not stifled. Rather, it is tempered by the wisdom of the ages."

I immediately recognised the tremendous value of the concept. Not long ago I had visited my dear grandmother in the aged care facility. I remembered the misery I saw there. I came away feeling ill at the thought of all those senior citizens who had outgrown their usefulness in our high-tech society. All those talented minds filled with knowledge and experience, were resigned to sitting around in easy chairs, discarded by their families and waiting to die. It was such a waste of wisdom.

As the heavy wagon bumped along the cobblestone road, I reflected on the age and quality of the teachers in our public schools. I recalled the many gripes my sister expressed about the education system and the concern she felt for her children. I also remembered the teary eyed attempts at discipline by a tiny young thing, scarcely as tall as myself, when I was in grade six or seven. At that moment, our university qualified teaching programme seemed grossly inadequate compared to the Yuwmahn's prevailing culture of personalised education by wise and loving members of their own family.

Other aspects of our education system, such as the large class sizes and crowded classrooms were not in evidence either. There were no classrooms or formal classes, only family gatherings of grandparents and little ones, of innocent smiles and grey-haired carers, of inquiring minds and dedicated teachers who loved their pupils more than life itself.

Of all the amazing components of this civilisation, the sight of small children learning at their grandparent's knee under the direction of their older generations was a powerful manifestation of the strength and importance of family. Most of the classes were held in their homes, although we passed several groups seated by the way on an excursion to observe some of the wonders of the world around them.

My mind jumped to the grandparents I knew back home who either rarely saw their grandchildren or were lumbered with them almost full-time because the parents worked such long hours. The grandparents of Yuwmah appeared to have the balance right, spending quality time with their young charges for a few joyous hours while the parents worked in the fields to support the whole family.

One such group was assembled in the central meeting area as we approached. They waved enthusiastically. The heavy wagon continued along the road and turned off into the grain store not far from my new abode. Inside were thousands of bags of flour piled almost to the rafters. This was without question a well-stocked grain store, which could feed the city for several years. The rich smell of freshly baked bread wafted on the midday breeze from somewhere nearby.

Kish jumped from the wagon and without hesitation began to unload the sacks. The driver and Pahoran did the same. The work ethic of these people was unmistakable. If something needed to be done, everyone pitched in and did what was necessary without thinking. The mindset of the shirker, so prevalent in my world, did not exist among these people. Everyone helped each other.

I immediately joined in, not only to keep up with them 'one-for-one', but to work harder than my companions in some vain attempt to prove my willingness and commitment to the common cause. I raised a considerable sweat as we manhandled the entire wagonload of freshly ground flour.

By the end, I was exhausted, but the towering sacks were evidence enough of our labours to leave me with a deep sense of achievement I hadn't experienced in years. When the task was completed, we stood for a moment to catch our breath and enjoy a job well done, and chatted on for a further hour thereafter. It was a bonding time that left me feeling an integral part of something of tremendous worth.

CHAPTER 7

We would never allow ourselves to flirt with the forbidden.

As the heat of the day came upon us, we farewelled the driver and headed off along the cobbled road in the direction of our abodes. Walking with a light and joyous heart, I found myself feeling very much at home. This morning I had qualified myself as a willing and worthy equal. There would be no monetary payment for my efforts, but I was surprised at how much my contribution meant to me. I felt a warm glow somewhere deep inside, in a place I was barely aware of.

I found Kish to be a friendly and easy-going fellow of about my own age. I enjoyed his company and our time together. Already we had established the basis of a firm friendship.

"So gentlemen, is there a tavern where we can stop off for a drink before we retire?" I asked with a suggestive smile.

Pahoran squinted his eyes. "You mean a place that serves alcoholic beverages, Mr Saomes?" he shot back in a concerned voice.

As I nodded my response, Kish lengthened his stride and turned toward me to draw my full attention.

"In Yuwmah we are free from the things of the world that cause great harm, Mr Saomes. We no longer make war with others, and neither do we make war with ourselves. There are no drugs or alcohol here. We shun such things and treat them as the poisons they are."

"We prefer to be sober and in full control of our thoughts and actions rather than to deliberately impair them. We find no joy or purpose in becoming intoxicated and 'out of it' or carrying on like silly giggling children! Mind-altering substances cause people to be less than they could be. Instead, we choose to be at our best, at our strongest and sharpest always, and strive to get high on pure happiness."

Following his lead, Pahoran broke in. "The natural highs we feel as we live a purposeful life are far more mind-blowing than any drug-induced condition, Mr Saomes! Our parents teach us from a young age that we must never flirt with the forbidden. We do not allow ourselves to consider anything that is potentially dangerous or debilitating. Would you allow a child to stand on the edge of a precipice and look down, knowing full well that a simple stumble may cause their total destruction? Alcohol and other such substances dull the senses, blur the judgement, and limit one's capacities. Under their influence we are never at our best. Even small amounts impair our faculties, change who we are, and weaken our resolve for right and good."

"Worse than this," continued Kish, "such substances have the potential to take control and turn us into creatures who are without redemption. It is not only a matter of being rendered shameless or useless. Our behaviour under their influence often impacts adversely on others, especially in relationships with family and friends, because such substances generally bring out the worst in us. We in Yuwmah find no justification for such things in our community or in our lives. In the outside world they are the root of much misery and despair, and one of the major causes of regret and sadness."

Pahoran came back with added enthusiasm. "Above all, it is such a fine line between us controlling them, and them controlling us. In fact, many people think they are conducting themselves acceptably as they partake, but far too often this is not the case. They need to understand that we only control those substances until they begin to control us: to speak for us, act for us, and eventually lead us into paths we would never go without them. They can so easily enslave us, and they may ultimately destroy us. We would never allow ourselves to be tempted by such things."

After a moment, Kish added, "There is a city nearby that allows and even encourages the consumption of alcohol, but it is not the kind of place I wish to visit.

There is much aggression and fighting, with ugly scenes that are most regrettable, especially for the children. Many social problems exist because people behave badly when under the influence." His voice tapered off to silence.

"In Yuwmah," added Pahoran, "we also shun other substances such as coffee and tobacco. Even artificial sweeteners and many preservatives are frowned upon because they have unpleasant effects on our mood and character. Caffeine, for example, is such a sinister substance. It enlivens our mind and gives us a kick along, but after the 'up' there is a distinct 'down', and each successive dose is one step closer to addiction and eventual burn-out."

"In the western world, when the mind demands rest it has become customary to take stimulants to enhance short-term performance, but this causes considerable long-term harm. As the effects of the drugs wear off, many find themselves almost unable to function. At this point some turn to other more damaging substances. When people wake feeling washed out and exhausted, many turn to stimulants to get themselves going. Once they reach such extreme behaviours, they are on a downward road to imminent self-destruction."

"Many enter into heavy drug addiction by embracing socially acceptable drugs, like caffeine and painkillers which are supposedly harmless. Eventually though, people may turn to stronger substances to give them the jump-start they feel they need. With reliance comes addiction. Once people embrace the practice of turning to any form of drug to affect their mood or performance, it is a small step to more potent substances which hold far darker consequences."

Kish nodded. "Can you imagine a world without drugs, Mr Saomes? What a different world it would be. The police and support services could be halved and more. There would be far less violent crime, fewer accidents and deaths on the roads, less domestic and social violence, less poverty, depression and mental illness, and less divorce. Most of all, fewer children would have reason to be sad or disappointed by those they rely on."

As we approached our abodes, I considered the full picture of a world without the menace of the drug culture. I had always held the opinion that if people wanted to affect their brain with substances that alter who they are and how they feel—then it was up to them—as long as their choices didn't impact negatively on innocent bystanders.

But invariably their choices did have an impact, and all too often lives are lost or ruined. I thought of all the crime attributed to drug addicts to feed their habit, and all the drunk drivers, or those whose reflexes were too dulled to prevent an accident. I thought about the fools people make of themselves when they lose their normal inhibitions, and all the sadness and conflict when people cease to be sensitive to others.

My face contorted as I considered the problems drugs brought to families, especially those who were forced to watch as loved ones slowly destroyed themselves. I'd never been one who promoted blanket abstinence of anything, but I could certainly appreciate the Yuwmahn stance against mind-altering substances.

I was also acutely aware from my own experience that even a small amount of alcohol caused a rollercoaster of emotions. First the normal inhibitions began to flee, and the chatter increased, followed by loud laughter and silliness. Then came the serious phase. As emotions intensified, people became argumentative and aggressive, then melancholy and introspective. The following day they were subdued and less inclined to be light-hearted. Some were harsh and abrasive, or snappy and critical, and people steered clear of them.

The Yuwmahns wanted to be at their best always, not to compromise themselves or others. Clearly their desire not to make war with themselves was a worthy ideal. Indeed, I remembered the words of my own father on this subject, "You don't have to dance with the Devil. There are always better partners and smarter options."

"To the Yuwmahn mind, human life is precious and full of purpose," said Kish. "It is something to be cherished, honoured, and celebrated. Life in the west has such little value or meaning. By Yuwmahn standards, you live in a temporary and self-destructive society, Mr Saomes. Not only do people regularly harm each other—they also harm themselves. The freedom to choose the higher path, and to openly pursue one's greater destiny is prized highly here. The right to be without dangerous distractions is one of the greatest triumphs we have achieved as a people."

I've since come to realise that in every western society there is a degree of self-destructive behaviour. As a result, there is also an underlying element of fear— but not here. These were gentle and innocent folk who lived without concern for hidden dangers. There were no secretive behaviours for self-preservation and no aggression or submission in their voices or actions. As a social group, everyone seemed open and comfortable.

There was no sign of class distinction in Yuwmah either, or any form of force or compulsion. Women and the elderly were treated with the utmost respect, because the men were raised to be gentlemen. Even the young beamed with self-confidence and a quiet sense of self-worth. I saw no pressure upon them to conform in ways that might be unpleasant. In fact, unlike many of the youth back home, there was no insecurity or hesitation in their actions or uncertainty in their eyes. They showed enormous respect for their parents and family, yet there was no bowing or any sense of inferiority. Everyone held their heads high, and all were so very mindful and considerate of others.

Back at my abode, I realised how at ease I was here. I was sure no one was 'out to get me' or take advantage of my ignorance. If I needed anything, I was confident anyone would help as best they could. How remarkable! But more than this was the profound feeling of safety and security. I felt no fear and no sense of needing to be on guard. There were no dark corners where evil lurked, and neither was there darkness in the countenance of the people. No one carried keys because there were no locks. Security was not an issue. As I retired for the midday nap, my front door was unbolted.

My mind was too active to sleep, so I took my pen and continued to make notes:

"We value all that God has given us," Kish had espoused, "from the sunrise to the sunset, to the moon and stars that shine down and inspire us. We respect the seasons and the variety they bring. We appreciate the air we breathe, and daily express our gratitude for the strength and capacity to breathe it, for surely our God holds all things for the benefit of man in His caring hand."

"But above all, Mr Saomes, we appreciate our right to choose. We are not compelled or pressured in our daily walk. We choose who we will be and the path we might travel through this life of probation. In our infancy and youth we are guided by loving parents and family, but as we become worthy to choose for ourselves, we are given the authority to do so. The right to choose—to become the master of our own destiny, is the greatest of all freedoms and the most celebrated meaning of life."

I made a large asterisk beside that paragraph. This was a concept I hadn't considered before. In the west, we rarely make time for such reflection. With new insight, such considerations seemed immensely important and deserving of a more thorough investigation. I sat back on my bunk and stared into space. The thought of becoming the master of one's own destiny seemed a monumental leap from the chaos and calamity of daily life back home, where everyone answered to someone.

"Our abodes are not paradise, but they are the closest thing to a piece of Heaven we can create in mortality. In Heaven we will live in paradise if we are found good enough to enter. May we never forget that this world is for learning and developing the attributes of Godliness, to refine our imperfect character and prove ourselves worthy to enter the presence of He who created us. So, here we live in humility and await that great day which shall surely come to all who have done enough to return to our heavenly home and receive an eternal inheritance."

"The people of the greater world seek to enjoy the attributes and rewards of Godliness, but they give no thought to attaining them. They have correctly identified some of the desirable ends, but they have misconstrued the means of reaching them. They want security and untold wealth and happiness beyond measure, but they fail to see that such can be found in the simple things of life."

"They seek for grand mansions, money and power, but such things lead only to deeper feelings of insecurity and spiritual poverty, and always to frustration and sadness. The example set by the Divine One reflects a simple and uncomplicated life filled with love, service, and personal refinement. Continual and ongoing progress is a more excellent way to a rewarding and happy life than any form of self-indulgence or drug induced euphoria, or any other thing man might try to substitute."

At this concept I shuddered. If anyone had spent their life in self-indulgence and the pursuit of pointless pleasures, it was me. Was anyone more aware than I of the emptiness or the lack of fulfilment that stems from seeking riches and material things? At that pivotal moment I examined the depths of my soul, and perhaps for the first time saw a clear portrait of my true self.

In spite of my recent revelations, I sat at the massive table and ate from the fresh crusty loaf with a satisfaction I had not felt before. Today I had contributed to the making of other life-giving loaves, and others would eat bread in the future because of my small yet significant efforts.

In the silence of the afternoon, I looked around me. I could almost hear the sounds of children playing, just as I had witnessed this morning. I could imagine the smiles of satisfaction on the faces of family members seated opposite me, feeling their ghosts all around as I sat in their midst.

I considered their contentment and the nature of their challenges. Families had once dwelt in this home, and for a brief moment I was aware of their presence. They were humble folk who drew simple pleasure from their uncomplicated lives. Perhaps the depth of their satisfaction was that 'special something' we've lost from the greater world; that elusive elixir of life that so many crave but can't seem to find.

I filled the tub in the private room and submerged myself in the pleasant pool. After a soothing soak I felt rejuvenated and filled with a new-found exuberance. Was this the 'reward of the just' that most of us only read about? I think perhaps it was.

CHAPTER 8

*True democracy is the best method of governance,
but to maximise its potential everyone should
find themselves in their own majority.*

After a brief midday nap, I sprang up quickly and pulled on my shoes. My mind was buzzing with questions for Mahonri. The city centre was a bustle of activity. I felt its energy as I made my way through the crowd. A small group of musicians played wooden flutes, giving the effect of birdsong through the trees as I approached.

Mahonri was sitting with his old friends beneath the canopy of green. From a distance I could tell they were enjoying themselves. I joined them eagerly and introduced myself to those I didn't know.

"Tell us of your morning, Mr Saomes," prompted Mahonri. "By the look on your face you've experienced much this day that has made you happy."

"Ah, what a day I've had gentlemen!" I exclaimed. "I walked along the wall from the south gate to the west gate," I gestured, waving both hands in opposite directions. "You are indeed an industrious and highly organised community, and I'm extremely impressed by what I've seen. Your people are incredibly resourceful."

"And what have you concluded about where you might be employed, Mr Saomes?" asked Mahonri.

"I was so taken by what I saw that I haven't stopped to consider where I might fit in. Is there a particular area where labourers are few?" I asked. "I'd be happy to join in wherever I'm needed."

"Very good, Mr Saomes," said Mahonri with obvious satisfaction. "We are not short of workers anywhere, but I know your efforts would be appreciated in the gathering of wood for our fires. Winter has passed and our supplies are low. You would be doing the city a great service should you apply your labours there. If gathering wood might suit you as a worthy endeavour, I shall make the necessary arrangements."

"That sounds fine," I replied. "This morning I helped to unload a wagon laden with bags of flour at the grain store, and while I am a little stiff around the shoulders, I must admit it did me good. I found it challenging and extremely satisfying. Cutting wood may have the same benefits," I smiled.

"Ah, Mr Saomes," replied Mahonri, "I fear that tomorrow you may be even stiffer around the shoulders! Indeed, you may feel some discomfort in other places as well!" he chuckled. Others at the table joined in the light-hearted ribbing, causing me to feel somewhat embarrassed by my lack of fitness.

"We do not laugh at you, Mr Saomes! We only laugh with you, and at ourselves. Each of us knows all too well what you shall feel, but we hope in the end it proves beneficial. You have contributed to the betterment of our community, so the discomfort you suffer may be much like a man's perspective of childbirth. You will experience the pain of bravely facing what must be endured, but you do not shirk your role or let your opportunity pass. Your efforts are commendable."

"As for me," commented an older grey-haired man named Abuti, "I would rather unload a dozen wagons than give birth just once." A quiet chuckle broke out around the table. "Even a hundred wagons!" exclaimed another. In reply Mahonri muttered something under his breath in his own language and the whole group roared with unabated laughter. I had no idea what was said, but I got the general picture. I could see it was going to be quite an afternoon!

A basket of rhubarb appeared on our table and we began to chop the fresh red and green stems into bite-sized pieces. The chore was over in a moment, but as the basket was removed, another appeared full of carrots. I found the Yuwmahn attitude to food admirable. There was a certain sacred appreciation of every morsel. The off-cuts and peels were handled as carefully as the edible parts. Not a single piece was lost or eaten.

"How did your history lesson go today," I enquired of Mahonri.

"Ah, my history lesson. How do I say this?" he replied with an uncertain smile. Several of the others chuckled at his manner and expression, or perhaps they knew what was coming. "I have mixed emotions, Mr Saomes. When I told the children about the great siege, no one believed me! My little great-granddaughter told me it was a most disgusting story!" he continued to further laughter.

"We are sorry, Mr Saomes. You have no idea why we are laughing. We must seem like giggly children," exclaimed Kish. "Although some of us are worse than others!" he said as he shot Abuti a broad accusing smile.

"At least we don't smell bad!" Abuti replied. As the commotion settled, Mahonri continued in more sombre tones.

"Over a thousand years ago a tribe of invaders descended from the north and encircled our city. They were fierce warriors with swords and spears and heavy armour. We had no desire to go into battle against them because they numbered many, so we posted our archers along the wall and kept them at bay by showering their advances with clouds of arrows."

"As the weeks passed, they must have thought we were close to starving inside these walls. But in truth, we could have lived for several years on the food stored in our warehouses. There was no danger of starvation. Each morning we proudly wafted the aroma of freshly baked bread over their hungry army in taunt; nevertheless, we were most annoyed at our state of siege."

"Finally, a wise old elder named Lamhi devised a plan to deliver our victory. At night, by the light of the half moon, a few brave warriors climbed down into the sewer and made their way out through the wall. They planted small barrels of gunpowder and piles of stones in rows across the fields, and marked them with sheaves. Then they returned as they had gone and rejoined their brothers in arms."

"But they smelled terrible!" interjected Abuti. "Several days passed before their wives could go near them!"

Mahonri continued, "The next morning before sunrise, our enemies gathered to come against us in strength. But before they ran across the fields shouting their bloodthirsty cries of war, a single Yuwmahn warrior climbed up on each of the four walls and prayed aloud. 'Oh God, we are a peaceable people. Therefore, will you send down thunder and lightning, that our unworthy adversaries might know that you, who has all power, do fight with us against them.' "

"This angered our enemies, even though they had no knowledge of our God. Neither did they have knowledge of gunpowder. As they advanced across the fields, our archers took aim and shot a barrage of blazing arrows at the barrels. Lightning and thunder exploded all around. In panic our enemies turned about and ran for their lives to escape what they believed was the wrath of our God. Many were so frightened, they dropped their swords and spears as they fled."

"And what splendid implements of war they were!" bellowed Abuti. "Our soldiers gathered them up as they pursued the fleeing mass and slew the enemy with their own weapons. Victory was ours, and each year we celebrate with a great festival in remembrance. And from that day to this, no one has ever gone down into the sewer again!"

It was a comical conclusion to a remarkable story. I marvelled at the ability of this humble people to rise up and fight against injustice, to battle and slay the enemy for their own protection. As I looked around the table, I saw that by nature they were gentle and peace-loving, but I also saw in their eyes the capacity to be brave and warlike. They were a proud people who would defend their city, their families, and their freedom with a ferocity and vigour that few could match.

"Our history is full of stories of war, Mr Saomes. Until the Divine One came among us and established peace we were a warlike people who lived and died by the sword. We spent our days in pursuit of the spoils of war and fought to possess anything we desired."

"It sounds a very bloodthirsty and brutal way to live," I commented.

"It was our way, Mr Saomes," replied Mahonri. "It was all we knew. Each generation of children was raised to be soldiers, steeped in the art of combat and strategy."

"I believe a similar situation now exists among the gangs in some of the world's larger cities," commented Abuti. "And likewise, among many ethnic groups in war-torn nations."

"Oh yes," replied Mahonri before I could answer. "It is precisely the same today among them as it was with us several thousand years ago. The children learn the culture of their parents, so it is passed down from one generation to the next. Each successive generation becomes further desensitised, more battle-hardened and cruel."

"It is indeed unfortunate," said Abuti. "Perhaps one day they will learn of a better way. Although, the current social policy is focused so heavily on the rights of the individual that I fear they would have to go full circle before a solution can be reached."

I was taken aback. What was happening here? The Yuwmahns were commenting on current affairs, yet how could they possibly know of such things? This came as quite a surprise. While I regarded them as not being from the same world as me, obviously they felt differently.

I asked somewhat tentatively, "I don't understand your meaning. Do you disagree with the concept of individual rights and freedoms?"

"Not per se," replied Mahonri. "But when the rights of the individual or the few take precedence over the rights of the many, then clearly the system is out of balance and the pendulum has swung too far. When the law is set too much in favour of the individual, the multitude may be forced to tolerate all manner of preposterous ideals, which is exactly what is occurring all around the world."

I shook my head in confusion.

"I'll give you an example," said Mahonri. "In Yuwmah, we believe homosexuality to be a disgusting practice and a sin condemned by our God from the very beginning. Indeed, many like-minded countries around the world have legislated harshly against such practices for thousands of years, so we are not alone. But while we love all men irrespective of colour or creed, we do not always love or approve of their actions. So the question is posed, Mr Saomes, 'Should the majority be required by law to tolerate the behaviour of any such minority if they find their actions offensive or unacceptable?' "

"Like many other minorities in the greater world, the homosexuals protest their right to be different. They ask to be accepted as a 'legitimate and alternative lifestyle'. Yet, going back through the generations, mankind has consistently found their actions to be abhorrent to such a degree that they were treated with extreme disdain. In many places, they were put to death because of the depth of disgust felt by the majority towards them."

"So who is right here; or rather, who has the right here? Should the majority be compelled by law not to discriminate, and thereby find themselves having to tolerate a minority whose practices they find disgusting? Or are the majority within their rights to speak up and openly condemn those they find unacceptable, even to cast them out if they feel to?" asked Mahonri.

I grimaced as I struggled to weigh justice from both sides. "So by what you're saying, a minority should not have the right to offend the majority?" I replied.

"Of course!" said Mahonri. "That is true democracy. If the majority don't like the actions of the few, or if they are offended by them, they shouldn't have to put up with them. And they should be allowed to openly express their opinions, irrespective of media bias and social engineering to the contrary. However, the forces of humanism are gathering momentum around the world, and they are devious and sly, so change will shortly follow because their foothold is significant."

"At the moment, the homosexuals of the world, along with dozens of other sub-cultures, cry loudly that their human rights are being abused because the majority disapproves of them. But what of the human rights of the majority to live without the unpleasantness of those they perceive as misfits, fringe elements, or degenerates?"

"Not only is the call for anti-discrimination a very socialist doctrine and completely undemocratic, but the simple idea that the greater majority should be forced to tolerate the unpleasant actions or consequences of a few deviants is ludicrous."

"As for me," said the older man, "I don't like brussels sprouts either. But I don't fear them, and I certainly don't have a phobia about them! I simply don't like them—and claim the right to openly say so."

"But really, the best solution to this hideous dilemma is quite straightforward," continued Mahonri. "Let those who are different dwell somewhere else where their behaviour is not unacceptable to those around them. Let the homosexuals form their own community where they can live in harmony with other like-minded people. Let the white supremacists or any other colour or creed live in a segregated society if they want, and let those who are happy to live in a multicultural community do so as well. Such a situation would see the democratic process at its simplest and best."

"We wish those who are unacceptably different no harm if they cause us no problem, and we accept their right to choose to live in their own way. If we allowed all those who want to play loud music after midnight to gather in one place away from those who are offended by such noise, then where is the harm? But we must never have a situation where any minority is holding the majority to ransom, or where the rights of the many are violated by the rights of the few."

"Exactly," said Abuti. "True democracy is the best method of governance, but to maximise it we need to have everyone in their own majority. So it becomes a simple exercise to allow the different groups to have their own space and govern themselves within it. If the democratic nations would only take the extra step to give minorities their own place to be, we could produce any number of harmonious societies—free to enact their own local laws and take democracy to a whole new level."

"The key to allowing everyone to live in peace and harmony is to remove the force. If no one is forced to live in a situation or under a law they don't agree with—isn't that the key to living in peace? Here in Yuwmah, we find the concept of a blended world quite absurd. It seems ridiculous to us that the many should be forced to tolerate those who are different to the point of being offensive."

"Likewise is the absurd idea that one set of rules should exist for everyone within a particular country and all around the world, without allowing for cultural or individual differences. In future, if they are successful, the dictators will create untold social problems by introducing policies of forced integration and mass obedience."

"We in Yuwmah find it fundamentally wrong that any majority should be expected to accept anything they would rather not tolerate to appease the extremes of just a few. We frown upon the concept of trying to make every nation and locality the same. Let the world be a diverse and interesting place. We can't allow the masters to force every town and village to be a socialist clone of everywhere else."

"But for now, the whole world is being pulled under one legal umbrella called 'international law', and to touch on an old adage, all the eggs are being placed in one basket. The prevailing legal imperative being forced into the statutes of every country towards a 'one world government' is a prime example of the few dictating unacceptable terms to the many. Such a divisive social system is destined to cause ongoing problems."

"This concept of a singular 'global village' does not promote a unified and harmonious society, Mr Saomes. Quite simply, irrespective of the various beliefs and customs around the globe, if we are to find universal peace, the will of the people must be heard and the voice of the majority must be upheld in every region."

As evening closed in, the people began to disperse and head for home. Mahonri walked with me along the cobblestone road, savouring the cool breeze. When we reached my abode, Mahonri stopped and lightly gripped my arm.

"Mr Saomes, tomorrow is our Sabbath, so we spend the day in personal prayer and contemplation. We do not assemble as we have in previous days. We also fast until the evening meal. Only the children are fed through the day. No one works tomorrow. Water is pumped and the gates are guarded, but they are closed. No one may come or go on the Sabbath. It is our day of rest from the things of the world and our time of worship."

"If it pleases you, Mr Saomes, in the morning my wife and I should very much like you to accompany us to church. And afterwards, I have sought permission from my father and mother for you to join our family for the afternoon. Does my proposal meet with your approval?" asked Mahonri humbly.

"I would be honoured to accompany you," I replied, "and especially honoured to meet your family."

"Very well, Mr Saomes. So shall it be. Until tomorrow then. We shall call for you at mid-morning."

I nodded my agreement and Mahonri gave a small bow and a soft smile as we parted.

Through the sky-window, the stars were now coming out in all their heavenly brilliance, so clear and bright that I could almost reach up and pluck one with my bare hands. It was a magical night and a fitting conclusion to another unforgettable day.

CHAPTER 9

We can make our homes a piece of Heaven if we choose to.

Sleep came easy in Yuwmah. As I rose from my bed I felt refreshed. My body was invigorated and acclimatising well to the new environment. I sucked in the early morning air and exhaled expansively.

In the night I had dreamed of marriage, of all things! My high school sweetheart and I were standing side by side in the gathering place. Mahonri had performed a solemn and beautiful ceremony. As newly-weds we retired to my humble abode to begin our life of wedded bliss as husband and wife. In the light of day my dream turned into a nightmare, for in recent years that wisp of youthful perfection had hardened considerably from the struggles of a most unfortunate life. Perhaps if she'd married me instead of that wimpish waste of good air who was once my friend, her life might have been easier and more fulfilling. What a thought!

I was unsure of when they might come for me, so I quickly prepared myself. No one was concerned about the exact time here. There were no clocks or wristwatches or any form of precise timekeeping that I could see, yet everyone was always on time.

Feeling peckish, I checked the small cupboard, but there was no crusty loaf to be found. Then I remembered the day of fasting observed by the entire city and decided to curb my appetite. My searching though, led me to understand the appearance and disappearance of the food. There was a small chute through the front wall that allowed some kind soul to deposit and remove a tray, much like the old-time motel room service.

I was now wearing the third of the three robes. The soiled two were hanging on their hooks in the parent's retreat. I wondered how they might be cleaned. After due consideration, I threw them in the tub and washed them with a little soap, then rinsed and hung them to dry on their pegs.

Next I decided to unpack my gear, which sat unattended at the foot of my bunk. I took out the two-way radio and checked it. The lights glowed as expected and all seemed in working order. Tomorrow I would send a message to let my team know I was okay and give them an idea of when I might be ready to leave.

As I began to tidy up, I found myself pondering how much more there was to learn about these incredible people. I took out my voice recorder and considered where to capture some audio. My camera also lay silent and beckoning. On a clear day I would take a swag of shots, but that was for later. For now, my mind was too absorbed with finding out more.

The bag of plastic trinkets lay untidily beside my heavy boots and smelly socks. As the contents of the pack found a semblance of order, I realised what a messy character I was. I wondered what the people of this meticulously clean and well-kept city might think of an untidy swine such as I? Perhaps they would cast me out to dwell in the wilderness with the other animals who never washed their socks or tidied their rooms!

"We all need someone to keep us focused, to prompt us to attend to the things we would prefer to leave for another day, Mr Saomes. A good woman would teach you to be a better man." I could hear Mahonri's gentle voice instructing me. "She would alert you to be more selfless and patient, and bear you children who would teach you more about yourself than you could ever learn on your own. Children have a particular way of making us aware of our imperfections and helping us to see the kind of man we must become if this life is to be of benefit to our future beyond the grave."

Mahonri often sounded like my mother, but I wasn't game to tell him so. He also sounded wise and all-knowing—so much so that at one stage he almost had me convinced I was missing out on the most wonderful aspects of life by remaining single.

"Perish the thought!" I laid back on the bunk with notepad and pencil to make a few jottings and perhaps find a beginning to my story of this remarkable journey. How would I begin? What would I say that could possibly explain all I had experienced? Should I do a series of articles about different aspects of the Yuwmahn culture and religion, or would a short story be a better way to express the astonishing things the world most needed to hear?

Prior to coming here, I envisioned a simple piece about the discovery of an unknown society that lived a primitive existence in the middle of nowhere, whose ignorant and uncomplicated lives could be told in just a few thousand words.

This project appeared straightforward when I agreed to it, and more to the point, my thoughts were shared by everyone on the team. How could I go back and suggest that they were the primitive ones? How do you begin to propose such a thing to wealthy high-tech city dwellers in a first world country such as Australia!

To be quite frank, would anyone believe that a more superior civilisation than ours could exist in a hitherto unexplored land? How does one tell his globe trotting colleagues that their lifestyle barely compares to the highly principled and disciplined Yuwmahn way, which places happiness at the core of everything they do? If only the whole team had shared my experiences these last few days. How shocked they'd be to know I was laying on this unusual bunk dressed in funny robes, waiting for my escorts to take me to church of all places!

As I stared at the blank page, my mind drifted in sombre contemplation. Mulling from thought to thought I was struck by the realisation that I had no idea what constituted 'worship' among these people. I was waiting to take part in something of spiritual significance—but what exactly? Today could be very interesting and uplifting, or it could be quite senseless and ridiculous. It might even be shocking.

I thought of the many strange rituals and practices in the name of religious observance around the world. There was such a multitude of ways to worship deity among the thousands of different churches, from chanting and dancing, to leaping and bowing before stone idols, wailing at a wall, or kissing a Pontiff's ring.

Perhaps I would have to wear a small cap or a string of beads. I might witness people dressed in elaborate robes adorned with priceless jewels or splendid headdresses of feathers or peaked hats, parading themselves before the peasantry who would prostrate themselves motionless upon the ground as they passed. Maybe there would be pageantry re-enacting the Divine One's birth or crucifixion, where a crown of thorns is forced on some poor soul's head until blood pours down their face.

The variety of worship was almost endless. I pondered why this might be so. If there is one God in Heaven, why is there not one method to worship?

Perhaps there is one right way and many wrong ways, but how does one know which is right or wrong? Is there one church that holds the truth and many churches that only claim to?

I thought of the scandal of the Church of the Red Rose ... or was it a purple camellia? Hundreds of young people flocked into the airports and bus terminals in some of America's larger cities, reciting a piece of scripture about love and peace to passers-by and offering them a flower for which they asked a donation. All the money went into some fat cat's pocket and every level of the operation took a cut along the way, except for those who did all the work.

I also thought of the television ministries, where for ten dollars your name could be included on a list, and people would pray for you as your name scrolled up their television screen. All of these contradictions gave a strange connotation to the word 'worship'. And what does worship really mean anyway? The concept was lost to me as I tried to reconcile all the activities and inconsistencies into one solitary word.

The firm sound of knocking brought me back to reality. I was about to find the answers to all my questions and more. The time had come to go to church!

I opened the door to find a beaming Mahonri accompanied by his lovely wife Misha. Her timeless face shone with a radiant and welcoming smile, reminding me of my dear grandmother, although I'm sure Misha was much older.

"I am very pleased to meet you, Mr Saomes," she said, bowing her head meekly. "My Mahonri has told me much of his time with you. He describes you as a gentleman of honour—a rare compliment from our people to anyone from the outside world!"

"He is very kind," I said, addressing my remark as much to Mahonri as to his beaming wife. I wanted to say more but words escaped me. Both gleamed with approval. We headed off along the road past the row of dwellings against the inside wall. People of all ages greeted us as we passed. On the other side of the street were parklands with large stone tables set among the trees, a far better idea than the small backyards in the suburbs back home.

As we walked, the sonorous chime of church bells filled the air.

"The bells call us to assemble," said Mahonri. "Everyone from our quadrant of the city is called to church. Did you hear the bells earlier?" he asked.

"I believe I did," I replied, "although I must admit I am not exactly sure. I slept well last night and long into the morning!"

"That is very good," said Misha. "Sleep is for the healing and rejuvenation of the body and especially of the spirit."

"And are you satisfied with your humble accommodation, Mr Saomes?" enquired Mahonri. "I have been meaning to ask you of this."

"My accommodation is more than adequate, thank you," I replied.

"Excellent," said Misha. "A person must feel secure and comfortable at home or their soul will not rest as it should. If the people of the greater world beautified their homes and fortified them against the ways of the world, they would find so much more happiness. We can make our homes a little piece of Heaven if we choose to, Mr Saomes. In such homes we learn the principles of Heaven, even to develop a more God-like character and enjoy a Godly peace."

"How true," I replied. "How true."

"In my home, I am queen and my Mahonri is king!" she continued laughingly. "Do you have fond memories of your youth and the home you came from, Mr Saomes?"

"Some," I replied in guarded tones. "Life was often difficult, but we had our happy times, I suppose."

"Oh, your poor mother!" replied Misha. "I wouldn't want to be a woman in the greater world. Here in Yuwmah though, life is far more stable and rewarding, and women are treated with absolute respect. Our society recognises that men and women are fundamentally different. Men are obviously bigger and stronger, yet from an early age they are taught by their fathers to respect their mothers who gave birth to them, and to appreciate the sacredness of womanhood. From their mothers they learn to be at their gentle best, to care for our women with honour and love."

"I hope you will not be disappointed that the proceedings of the church service will be in our own language, so you may not understand all that is spoken," said Mahonri apologetically.

"I'm sure it will be enough for me just to be there and observe," I replied.

At my comment, Mahonri and Misha gave a smile and bowed their heads together. I'm not sure what my words meant to them, but my reply seemed acceptable, which pleased me. We soon arrived at a simple building that was not as I expected. It was a stunning structure with a single spire reaching up to Heaven, set solidly over the entrance. But otherwise, it was strangely bare of the usual religious adornments. Gilded domes, statues, crosses, and stained glass windows portraying biblical images were nowhere to be found.

All around us were families. There were young parents carrying babies accompanied by grandparents who fussed over children and their own ageing parents. In one group I suspect there were six generations together. I was touched to see that even the very old held hands with their spouse as though they were young lovers.

We approached the door and filed respectfully inside. What followed was a simple service, devoid of the pomp and ceremony often on display in churches around the world. After the congregation partook of a sacrament of bread and water, several people spoke from the pulpit. I sensed that the presentations were informative and uplifting, and perhaps even inspiring, although the details eluded me.

At the conclusion of the service, the congregation stood and filed out, renewed and revitalised by the messages and the heavenly music. There were smiles, handshakes, and hugs all around. For some who attended, it may have been little more than a time of religious reflection, yet to me it was a moving experience that was difficult to describe.

Once outside, Mahonri introduced me to the older couple who were seated beside us. As I suspected, they were his parents, whose home I would visit that afternoon. I a lso met one of Mahonri's sons, Gen, who proudly introduced me to his wife Mina, their three sons and their wives and children. As we walked homeward, I talked with Gen and Mina about Yuwmahn families and learned that following the last great war, the size of the ideal family was set at seven children because of the shortage of men. The number was later reduced to five and now stood at two or three children per couple.

"Just the right amount to maintain a steady population," came his final comment. How they achieved this was not discussed, but I agreed with the principle that people should self-regulate their population to the needs of the community.

We also discussed the church service, at which point I asked the fundamental question, "Why do Yuwmahns attend church?"

"There are two main reasons we attend each week," Gen began. "The first is to partake of the sacrament and recommit ourselves to the principles of our religion. We do not 'eat of the body' or 'drink of the blood'—a horrid translation of the wording in scripture, and not what the sacrament is really about. We partake of bread and water in remembrance of the sacrifice made by the Divine One. He took upon Himself the sins of all mankind that we might be forgiven of our sin if we sincerely repent. In partaking the sacrament, we recommit ourselves to living a life which is pure and undefiled," he concluded.

"The second reason we assemble is to listen to the speakers, so that we might be strengthened in our commitment to those eternal principles. If there is a third reason, it is probably to come together with like-minded believers, to share a spiritual experience and to be part of something special. We also sustained officers and teachers who carry out the programmes and functions of the church."

We settled around the stone tables in the parkland opposite Mahonri's parents home. Several women entered the house and brought out baskets and platters of food for the children. None of the adults ate a single bite.

I found the afternoon fascinating as I met and mingled with several generations of this fine family. I was moved by the way the elderly sat at the centre and the younger generations came forward in an orderly manner to spend time talking with their forebears. The youngsters obviously afforded their elders the utmost honour and respect.

CHAPTER 10

'Is there a God who created us?'
is the most important question we could ever ask.

Mahonri's father, Melesch, was indeed an old man, yet he retained his mental agility and a laugh like none I've had ever heard! He also had piercing eyes that looked deep into my soul with every glance.

His most outstanding attribute was his voice. It was not a loud voice, and neither was it a strong voice, yet it penetrated to somewhere deep inside me, and I found myself wondering if this was how God might speak. He was undoubtedly the most Godlike man I'd ever met. Most of all, there was a presence about him—a powerful aura emanating from his person that held me speechless and in awe.

"Have you come to know our God, Mr Saomes?" Melesch asked in a commanding tone. I was taken back by the directness of his question, feeling his probing eyes looking deep inside me as though he could read my every thought. After a moment he must have discerned the little there was to know and began to speak, drawing me into his oratory like a small child.

"The greatest question we can ever ask, Mr Saomes, is such because the answer is fundamental to all things. 'Is there a God who created us?' If our answer is a definite 'no', we can eat, drink, and be merry until we die because nothing else really matters. But I think when we earnestly make this inquiry, something inside each of us speaks to our soul as if by the sound of our own voice, telling us there is more to mankind than this tabernacle of clay and our selfish animal nature."

"So, if the response to the question is anything other than an absolute 'no', other questions arise that demand answers. If we decide there is the slightest possibility that a God might exist, we must consider our relationship to Him. I have struggled with such questions all my life, Mr Saomes, and perhaps I have come to understand at least a few possibilities."

"Across the world today, most of mankind seeks to know their God as people have from the beginning of time. But in the west, because of the ongoing humanist influence, it has become quite populist and commonplace to deny His existence. But as we know all too well, when man is forced to face death or deep suffering, inevitably he turns to prayer."

"I feel to share a few thoughts with you if I may, because one day we may meet again in the hereafter, and

I wouldn't want you to greet me with any hint of—'Why didn't you warn me when you had the opportunity?' I also believe I will be called to account for my time here on earth. I don't want to be found guilty of being lax in my duty to warn my fellow man about something so important. Though, the main reason I want to share what I have come to understand is that I find the ideas so very beautiful! There is nothing more perfect than simple truth, Mr Saomes!"

After a brief pause for breath, the ageing man began to instruct me in earnest:

"Our God is the father of the spirit within us. Our spirit is as the breath of life to our mortal body. When the spirit enters our body prior to our birth, we become a living soul. When that spirit finally leaves, or our body is no longer able to sustain itself, we die, and our body quickly decays and becomes as the dust of the earth from whence it came."

"I hope you will understand, Mr Saomes, that our physical bodies are no more than receptacles for our spirits to dwell within. Spirit is a substance finer than our mortal eyes can discern, and the spirits of the dead are all around us. In mortality, it's as though a veil is cast over our eyes that we can't see through, but the spirits can see us. Our kindred dead watch over us and serve as angels to care for us. They will prompt our minds and guide our choices throughout our lives, if only we will listen and take heed."

"Because our God is the father of our spirits, which were born in Heaven, we refer to Him as our

Heavenly Father, because we also have earthly fathers of our physical bodies. And where was there ever a father without a mother, Mr Saomes?"

"We also have an elder brother—the Divine One, who paid the price to save us from the eternal consequences of our sin. He took upon Himself the sins of the world and opened the way for us to be forgiven if we will only repent of our iniquities and return to them no more."

"The Divine One is the eldest spirit to be born of our heavenly parents. But in a miraculous way, our God was also the father of His earthly body, so the Divine One is literally the 'only begotten of the Father in the flesh'. And after His resurrection from the dead, He too became as God. He and the Father are one in purpose, but they do not share the same body, so they are separate and distinct beings."

"The third member of the Godhead is the Holy Ghost who remains in the form of a ghost or spirit. The Father has a body of flesh and bones as does the resurrected Divine One, but the Holy Ghost has not yet been born of woman on the earth and will be the last spirit to be so. His realm is among the spirits of the dead where he oversees all that pertains to that sphere."

"The Holy Ghost has all authority there under the direction of the Father, so He too is a God having all knowledge and all power within His designated role. He is also 'at one' with the Father and the Divine One, but they are separate and distinct from each other. The Father is overall and is the source of all authority."

"Our purpose here upon the earth, Mr Saomes, is to learn to become like our heavenly parents. We do this by making choices. Choices are placed before us every day, both large and small. When we choose wisely, we receive the natural consequences of our choice, and we also receive an added blessing of increased contentment. When we choose unwisely, again we are subject to the natural consequences of our choosing, and sadly the blessings that we might have received for a wiser choice are held back. If we persist in choosing unwisely, despite the many promptings which will surely come to us to do better, even those blessings we have already received will be taken from us."

"As we learn to choose the way to the greatest happiness, which is the supreme purpose of this life, we also learn to understand the concept of true happiness. In doing so, we learn to be more like our God. We learn to understand Him, to think and act like Him, and to be happy like Him. We see our God as our heavenly father—a perfect being, who once was as we are now."

"The principal reason we were born to this earth is to come to understand Him, to seek Him out, and learn to be like Him, just as He learned to be like His father before Him. Whether God actually exists as flesh and bone is immaterial to the proposition that we see Him as 'the perfect man'. Throughout our lives we strive to be more like Him. Our every aspiration towards greater happiness brings us closer to that concept of perfection—which we term Godliness."

"The people of the earth seek for contentment today as they have through the ages, but they will not receive such if they fail to live as they ought, according to the commandments given to us from Heaven. The Divine One taught us to be meek, gentle, long-suffering, and patient. When we manage to be so, we are greatly blessed. A depth of contentment will attend us that all the wealth of the earth cannot buy. But when we are proud, arrogant, harsh, impatient, and selfish toward others, we will not have peace in our soul, and we will not be truly happy."

"Of course, we also strive not to kill or steal or bear false witness, and to love our neighbour as ourselves, and treat everyone with compassion. These are the fundamental teachings and the basic commandments that underpin the laws of Heaven and all we hold to be worthy and right. If everyone would embrace these teachings and become unified by them, what a different world we might enjoy. There would be peace in every country, in every city, and in every home."

"Unfortunately, the peoples of the world have rejected His teachings and seek instead after their own happiness in their own way—but they cannot find it. When they cannot immediately gratify their unbridled wants, their hearts turn to anger like a spoilt child. Their anger fuels contention and war. They fight for wealth, power, and domination, but such things are fleeting and unrewarding. The peace that follows being fair to all and right before God is immeasurably desirable, Mr Saomes. When we achieve such a condition, we are truly rich."

Again I was taken aback. He had spoken so gently, yet so intently and with such power. I was touched by his absolute belief in every word he said. There was no doubt in his mind that these things were true and that these truths were more important to mankind than any other knowledge we could ever acquire.

I made my departure earlier than most from that happy family gathering, but as I walked home, my mind was overflowing with the proceedings of the day. I pondered the point that in this culture the men were expected to be the head of their family, but they only held that position with the support of their wives. In Mahonri's words, "Being the head of the home means that men are ultimately accountable to their God for the care they have shown their family. As you say in your country in times of grave difficulty, the buck stops with us, Mr Saomes. But please understand that being the head of the home is not a position of authority. It is merely a position of ultimate responsibility—for what kind of man, when faced with a threatening situation, wouldn't step up to battle rather than leaving the unpleasantness to his wife."

"Chivalry is still alive and well in Yuwmah, Mr Saomes. We honour our women here. Both husband and wife must be equally yoked and look to each other in all things. Each will have their respective tasks and areas of responsibility, but when something dangerous or unpleasant demands to be dealt with, it is the man who should automatically step forward into the line of fire to protect his loved ones. Do you agree?"

I had watched the husbands, wives, and children interacting and communicating throughout the afternoon, and I was pleased to see that everyone treated each other with respect and courtesy. Only the very young were unruly. By nature these little ones were as noisy and demanding as any child around the world. But as they grew older, they also learned better. This was the opposite to my perspective of the young ones back home, who became more unruly and less respectful with each passing year.

Laying on my bunk, I realised that the Yuwmahn concept of religion and religious observance wasn't a separate part of their life or a 'Sunday only' affair, but an integral component of their daily walk. Their beliefs called them to consider how they conducted themselves every minute of their lives so that each step of their earthly journey might be meaningful and of benefit.

Moreover, religion to the Yuwmahns was not a pretence of pomp or ceremony. Their God was not an incomprehensible vagary but the embodiment of human perfection and absolute truth. As such, the principles of Godliness inspired the people to be at their best in every aspect of their lives.

Unlike many religious types I've known, Yuwmahn beliefs were an integral part of who they were—not an optional extra they turned to when it suited them. As a result, they were naturally kind and considerate of one another, rather than selfish and obstinate. I found this idea compelling. Under such a God, everyone was made accountable to themselves for their own actions, and their level of godliness was directly measured by their happiness.

My last thought before falling asleep was of a comment expressed by one of Mahonri's grandsons, that even if God does not exist, we will do well to act as though He does. In his words, "Unless we keep to the ways of a perfect Heaven—we are lost. What mankind needs more than anything is a sense of divine purpose, for without a tangible link to the divine, we are as mere animals."

Much to my surprise, I identified with a God who was once as we are, who rose to perfection and Godhood by honing his ability to control himself until he overcame all things. Through the course of the day I had also received a vision of what life might become if everyone embraced such teachings; and in doing so, I realised aspects of myself and my own selfish and imperfect nature that had never occurred to me.

CHAPTER 11

The young need heroes and role models to inspire them.
When the prominent and respected falter,
the whole of society trembles.

The sound of heavy wheels rumbling over the hard earthen road broke the silence of a perfect morning. The distinctive clip-clop of the horse's hooves emphasised our slow progress as we made our way across the fields and out to the wooded area beyond. Today was a workday, and I was keen to get amongst the action.

For much of the early morning, I lay awake picturing myself toiling with axe and saw to fill the rickety old wagon with firewood. Passing through the open fields, I clutched at the handle of one of the heavy axes, moving my hands over the smooth timber and down to the shiny head, appreciating its exquisite craftsmanship. It was much larger than the axes from home, but I was feeling strong. Within me was an unspoken expectation that I was up to the vigorous task ahead.

After a rough and bumpy ride through the forest, we arrived at an area where several trees had been felled to dry out. The stocky frame of Abuti sat beside me. As we travelled, he explained how trees were selected and marked for timber, and only the off-cuts were used for firewood. Our job was to cut and split the leftover pieces.

Abuti also explained that when a large tree was removed, several young trees were planted in its place. Over the years, the smaller trees were thinned to make way for the tallest, strongest, and straightest. Abuti also explained how the leaf litter returned much carbon to the soil, making the Yuwmahn community 'carbon-negative'.

"We have no place among the polluters of the world," he boasted. "The more trees we grow, the cleaner the air we breathe. Global warming could be reversed in just a few years if every nation would only replace the trees they've removed!" he concluded.

I had never held an axe until that morning, but through the night I'd rehearsed my actions a thousand times in my mind. I was brimming with confidence, imagining my new job an easy activity to execute. When we finally stopped and dismounted, I moved to a long limb and lifted the heavy implement high above my head. But as I raised myself on tiptoes to thrust the axe downward, I felt a staying hand.

"Tut tut tut, Mr Saomes," cautioned Abuti, sounding alarmed. "I fear you are about to chop off your leg! May I instruct you?" he asked firmly with an encouraging look.

Somewhat offended by his interference, I nodded my reluctant compliance and handed him the heavy tool.

"We take the branch and lay it over the trunk of the tree," he began. "Then we raise the axe with one hand to the level of our eyes and let it fall upon the branch like so," he said. The axe chopped the small branch smoothly and cleanly. He moved the branch up with his other hand and repeated the motion. Again, it split easily.

"The axe is our friend, Mr Saomes," he said. "We must never raise it as if in anger. It is a finely balanced instrument, so we handle it with the greatest of respect. Furthermore, like so many things of life, if we do not treat it with the consideration it deserves, it has the power to become a weapon and turn on us like a viper, with dire consequences!"

"Even when splitting the bigger pieces, we allow the axe to do the work. We lift and guide the axe as it falls."

Abuti then placed a sawn length on its end at the centre of the log. This time he raised the axe above his head with both hands and guided it forward with the smoothest of actions to split the sawn length sweetly in two.

"Now you may try, Mr Saomes," he said, handing me the axe. Again, he stood a piece of sawn wood on the log, but as I raised the handle, he gripped my hands.

"As the axe falls, you must always ensure that the end of the handle is lower than the head, like so," he said as we slowly lowered the axe together until it struck the log. "If the head is lower than the handle," he continued, "and if you should miss your mark, can you see how the axe would more than likely strike you?" With a firm grip he stayed my hands at chest level and moved the heavy implement down in an arc that brought the head within a span of my leg.

"Above all, Mr Saomes, you must learn to love your axe and treat it with kindness, much like you would a small child. The axe is strong and formidable, but it must be guided wisely with a delicate balance of firmness and tenderness. When the axe is about to do as it should, release it and allow it to act for itself. When we learn to exercise just the right amount of control and the appropriate respect, our axe and our children will willingly work with us, and not against us."

Stepping back, he bowed his head slightly and gave me the broadest of smiles. My lesson was over, or perhaps that was only my introduction. Either way, I had learned much already. I set about my task as shown, and before long I felt the ease of the motion as I split several piles of sawn pieces.

"Do you feel its power, Mr Saomes?" asked Abuti as he came towards me with a large cup in hand.

"I'm beginning to," I replied.

"Each axe has its own rhythm. When you find the rhythm, you unleash the tremendous power it holds. A sword is a similar thing. Also the rifle, Mr Saomes. You must hold it just so—to allow it to shoot true." Again I nodded my agreement.

"Do you have a wife and children, Mr Saomes?" he asked.

"No, neither," I replied almost apologetically.

"Ah ... your time will come. And when it does, you must remember your relationship with the axe. For as you have learned to work with your axe, so must you learn to work with your wife and children."

I was speechless. The wisdom of these people was fathomless. Who else in the world could tie the subtler aspects of marriage and parenthood to chopping wood?

At mid-morning we downed tools and stood around the wagon to enjoy a brief rest and a bite to eat. It was a pleasant gathering in the midst of the forest, with gentle birdsong in the trees above. The men talked peacefully among themselves. I immediately noticed a distinct lack of crude and vulgar language that often accompanies such conversations among groups of men back home. This was a far cry from the callousness of the lunchroom at the office.

For some time we laughed and joked together as others gathered around, speaking freely in their own language. It was such a relaxed atmosphere until suddenly, out of the corner of my eye, I observed something I couldn't comprehend. I looked around for some explanation, but everyone smiled innocently as if Katu's actions were nothing out of the ordinary.

Katu was our group co-ordinator—a short, aging man seated nearby. Without warning, he had moved behind the wagon and removed a bow and arrow from a holster at the front. As he fitted arrow to bow, he knelt behind the wheel with a sense of urgency and prepared to shoot. After a moment, he leapt up and fired into the distance. The arrow flew fiercely through the air with a soft buzzing sound. I followed its flight and saw it sink with force into a large tree a good forty yards away.

As the arrow struck, a raggedy man sprang out from behind the tree and ran for his life. All around me the men rose up in unison and charged after the fleeing figure. Their blood-curdling war cry caused the woods to erupt, scattering birds and animals. I ran with the men for a short distance until they gave up their chase and turned back to the wagon. I stood baffled as the men passed me, panting deeply from their brief burst of aggression.

"You are puzzled Mr Saomes," Abuti asked.

"I certainly am. What was that about?" I asked.

"That man must have been cast out from one of the cities nearby. He may have brought us danger. Katu did not shoot to kill—only to scare him away. Our war cry was for a similar purpose."

"Oh, I see," I replied, still bewildered. "But why not show him some mercy and feed him?"

"He was cast out for good reason, Mr Saomes. We must respect those who enacted the punishment and allow the man to feel the full weight of the consequences of his actions," came the firm reply.

The stout figure of Katu walked by with his head lowered. Abuti acknowledged him with a clench of his fist as if to congratulate him for his bravery and excellent shooting.

"Thank you, my friend," he nodded to Abuti, "but I am saddened. I once knew that man. He hails from a nearby city. In fact, there was a time when I respected him greatly, although I was very young. I remember him as a courageous and uncompromising character who inspired many on the sporting field."

"I knew him too," replied Abuti, "and I played against several of his sons who were equally capable in the sporting arena. I feel for those who looked up to him because obviously their hero has fallen into disgrace. The young need role models to inspire them, Mr Saomes. When the prominent and respected falter, the whole of society trembles."

"Exactly," said Katu. "The world at large is constantly being shaken because so few are capable of controlling their actions or ambitions in an admirable way. I feel for the youth of the world. These are difficult times. They strive to make their own way because there are so few heroes and role-models."

"I agree," replied Abuti. "The young around the world are growing up in an age when almost nothing is stable or sure. Hollywood often promotes evil as good, and good as evil. There is little of any real value on their televisions and devices, and much that subtly corrupts and confuses. Children's television and electronic games are perhaps the worst."

"Social engineering is everywhere. The innocent youth are being led into all manner of iniquity and depravity, all in the name of entertainment," said Katu, shaking his head. "Work has lost its meaning, self-indulgence is rife, self-control is a thing of the past, and everyone just wants to be entertained and have fun."

"Young girls paint their eyes, lips, and nails, and do terrible things to their hair in some vain attempt to look more beautiful," he continued. "But their faces are harder and angrier than ever, giving them an appearance that is artificial and quite unattractive. Young men tattoo their arms and bodies, thinking they look tougher and more formidable on the outside, but they don't appreciate the need to develop a strength of character or a sense of compassion."

"But it's the prevailing legal system that is the most corrupting," continued Abuti. "In the greater world, children are made aware of their legal rights long before they are mature enough to understand or exercise such rights wisely. Children suing their parents is a terrible indictment of any society."

"I feel for the children too," I added. "They are so often used as pawns in divorce settlements and their fundamental right to be raised by a mother and father is rarely considered in custody issues. There is something precious in the eyes of innocent children.

I'm sure they don't deserve the sadness they sometimes suffer. Divorce is such an ugly thing."

"So true," murmured Abuti. "If only our friend had kept himself better. When those we admire set a poor example, the consequences flow on through the generations and manifest themselves in all kinds of unfortunate ways."

After another hour of chopping, we loaded the wagon and headed back to the city. Stopping beside the bakery next to the grain store, we stacked our cargo in a low-roofed shed against the outer wall. Then it was home for the midday rest.

I felt remarkably strong and muscular as a result of my efforts that morning, and it occurred to me that this was the very reason everyone should do some physical work. As I walked into my abode, I flexed my shoulders and chest with a sense of pride. The physical effort had surely done its job on me, and my sense of achievement was unmistakable. Both the concept and the execution were quite exhilarating, especially when the work had the practical outcome of providing food and heating for the entire city.

After a refreshing bath I dressed in a fresh robe and ate bread and honey with renewed satisfaction. I lay awake for some time with the thoughts of the morning running through my head. My last recollection was of a shabby man with raggedy clothes being chased through the forest by screaming, bloodthirsty Indians. I shivered as I remembered their spine-chilling war cry.

When I awoke, I winced with stabbing pain, as though someone had taken one of those heavy axes and plunged it deep between my shoulder blades. "Oh, dear!" I muttered. Apparently, I wasn't as fit as I thought! I could almost hear the cackling at the gathering place as I went limping and moaning to join the afternoon throng. Abuti will be delirious!

I freshened up and came back to life slowly. Other aches and pains made themselves known in strange places. But every stab of discomfort reminded me of my achievements that morning. My only prayer was that I wouldn't be reminded for too long.

CHAPTER 12

*In our culture we covenant to give ourselves to each other
for all eternity, so marriage is more than being together
'till death do us part'.*

I returned to my bedroom and looked at my pack at the foot of the bed. Any day now I was due to send a message to the team who were waiting back in civilisation. My thought brought a sudden smile. How would Mahonri and the others respond to such a comment? Back in civilisation indeed!

But—when I made contact, what would I say? My team were expecting me to return with them. What would they think if I told them I felt at home here and wanted to stay? Could I really find joy here for the rest of my mortal days? For a moment my mind opened to the possibilities, but I drew no conclusions.

I shook my head vigorously and decided I was probably suffering from the aftershock of my earlier efforts, so I postponed any decisions until I had a clear mind. Right now was obviously not the time.

When my thoughts finally found clarity, I was strangely convinced that life in Yuwmahn society was more enjoyable and rewarding than where I'd come from, and that going back may not be what I wanted. Whether I stayed a week or a month didn't matter to anyone. The money was in the story. I could remain here for as long as it took to get something down on paper, which would give me time to think deeper and with greater clarity.

With no thought of what I might say, I tried to contact the team. Their plan was a simple one: to search out relevant background information, take a thousand photos of local scenery and people, secure the permissions for publication from the relevant government authorities, and return home within the week. But then again, my inclusion in their return journey wasn't necessary as I had an open agreement with the shuttle company to collect me whenever I was ready.

As expected, my cell phone showed no signal, so I tried the two-way radio. The crackle of interference was loud, but there was no response to my transmissions. The designated range of the transmitter (infernal contraption that it was) should have been more than adequate. Perhaps the weather was bad over the horizon, or I needed to rig a longer antenna to throw a signal over the mountains. In frustration I pushed the delicate instrument clumsily back into the corner. "I will deal with you later," I said in disgust.

As we sat at the gathering place, I shared my earlier experience in the forest with Mahonri, including our comments about fallen heroes and the woeful effects on society as a result.

"Worthy role models are rare," he commented. "When we find them to be less than we thought, the situation can be difficult to deal with. This is particularly true of family members. We idolise them when we're small, but eventually we realise they are not perfect. As we get to know ourselves better, we must inevitably face the sad truth that at times we too are less than we might have been. Forgiveness of ourselves and others is such a necessary act."

"Families are vitally important to us here in Yuwmah," said Mahonri. "Even when they show themselves to be less than perfect, they are still our own flesh and blood. A family group is special because it is the most fundamental unit of our society. That is to say, families are the building blocks that make up our social fabric; not individuals," he continued.

"I hope you understand and are not offended when I say that individuals tend to be self-serving and contribute little compared to families who signify real strength. As a unit, family members learn to give much to receive little, and by sheer weight of numbers, families can be self-sufficient and self-regulating."

"Any attack on the family from the outside world should also be taken as an attack on society. Western society is crumbling rapidly because the strength of the family is being systematically eroded. We have no such problems here though. Because of the tremendous family support, marriage among the young is a very different concept than in your culture. Without the social support of families, it would be a sad case of 'children marrying children', and 'children having children', which is the saddest of all."

"Of course, our young people are encouraged to wait until they are sure before entering into marriage, to be certain they have chosen wisely. Most don't marry until they are in their mid-to-late teens."

"Do you have divorce here," I asked.

"On occasions it has been considered, but it is not a simple process," Mahonri reflected. "Our social system and our religion offer some splendid alternatives when couples lose their way."

"We are mostly monogamous here at present," he stressed. "In our culture, we covenant to give ourselves to each other for all eternity, so marriage is more than being together 'till death do us part' as in the west. It's a very different perspective and one that requires far greater dedication and commitment. To us, life and marriage are eternal concepts that extend beyond the grave. And in defence of such a concept, Heaven would not be heavenly if my sweetheart were not there with me," he concluded.

"Tell me of your marriage process," I began … but mid-sentence the weight of his previous comments struck me. "At present you are 'mostly' monogamous?" I gasped almost critically.

Mahonri began reluctantly, "There have been times when our men were decimated in war and numbered far less than our women, so the need arose to be plurally married for a time. I've come to believe that in many ways it is not an ideal situation, but it serves the purpose of allowing all women to be mothers and for each of them to have claim on a husband for their care and support. We have never had concubines or servants here—a practice we consider abhorrent and completely unacceptable."

"Under a plural marriage arrangement, every woman can enjoy the privileges of being wed if she desires. The husband should consider all wives equally, but the first wife has a place of pre-eminence over the others. It is she who chooses the second and third wives and so forth, and represents them to the husband when dialog is required."

"Quite simply, Mr Saomes, the arrangement is in place for the sake of the women, and is administered by them. The men do their best to take upon themselves the added responsibilities of extra wives and children, but they have little or no input in the day-to-day arrangements. But of course, if either the husband or the first wife does not wish to participate in such a programme, they don't. There can be no force or coercion involved. The husbands, the wives, and the single women, have a choice to participate in plural marriage or remain as they are."

"Everyone here is free to choose," Mahonri continued. No one is forced into anything they find unacceptable, except on occasion for the minority—but let them remember that the majority rules. That's how democracy works. But those in the minority on any particular issue are free to go elsewhere and form their own majority among those who are like-minded—which is the best outcome for everyone."

A barrage of thoughts ran through my head but I decided to hold back most of my questions until I'd considered them further. "So, how old must you be in Yuwmah to be married?"

"Age has very little to do with it," Mahonri replied. "When the parents think their child is sensible enough and has found a worthy partner, they permit the marriage to take place. Because we all know each other here, it is much easier. The parents of both the bride and the groom must approve the match. If they don't, there can be no union except by appeal to the Grand Council. Appeals of this nature are rare and the council can never overturn the expressed wish of any parent. In such cases the council may only intercede to make a petition to either family as they think best for the young people involved."

"As for the age, we have debated that issue many times in the past. The main ideal we hold to is that the bride and groom should be about the same age. We would never condone older men taking young girls as wives. We should also stress that the parents do not arrange marriages; they only approve them. As for a specific age—this should be considered on a case-by-case basis. But there is an obvious need to have a benchmark, I suppose."

"The Divine One gave us the guideline," Mahonri added. "He decreed that it should be among us as it was among his people, both then and now, whereby the minimum age of consent to marry was twelve years. Of course most twelve-year-olds are not interested in such things, and most do not marry until they are sixteen or older."

"It would seem that the Divine One himself married at an early age, for such is the tradition among his people, even today. He may well have raised a large family before his thirtieth year. We know nothing of his life from the age of twelve to thirty, but he may have seen his children married before he commenced his earthly ministry. In fact, many consider the record of the marriage feast at Cana to be an account of the Divine One's own wedding."

Katu had just joined us and now interjected boldly. "It has always been logical to me that the Divine One would have had to be married. How could he have any idea of the complexities of marriage and parenting unless he experienced them first-hand? And if he descended below all things as the scriptures indicate, and suffered more and worse than any other, then surely that is the most perfect description of what marriage can be!" he exclaimed with a wry smile.

At his comment there was much laughter around the table bordering on the irreverent. I had chosen not to be married for that very reason, having long ago concluded that I was far too self-centred to be a good husband, so I assumed that for me it would end badly. My ambition for work and travel took priority. There just wasn't room for another person in my busy schedule, and children would have made life impossible!

"Katu speaks a sad truth," commented Abuti. "A woman is indeed a peculiar creature, and doubtless they will say the same of us. Still, I don't know what my life would have been without my dear wife," he sighed.

"Try not to think about it, my friend," said Katu. "It will only depress you!"

"We have made light of a grave matter, Mr Saomes," interjected Mahonri after a period of frivolity. "Many of us here may need to repent and seek the forgiveness of our beloved wives for our unkind words," he continued as he jovially eyed those who had spoken.

"You can tell your wife whatever you like of our conversation," said Katu. "As for me, I'm not saying a word! Earlier today you called me brave, but when it comes to standing against the women—I am a total coward. To me, my own daughters are the most fearsome of all!"

"You see, Mr Saomes," said Abuti after a time, "that even though we strive to be sober and forthright, and we try to be more Christ-like in our daily walk, there is an element of mischief in all of us that is hard to conquer!"

"Perhaps it's just as well too," said Katu. "Life may be less satisfying if we cannot sometimes laugh at ourselves and those we love."

We enjoyed a hearty meal together as we talked of many things. I was impressed with the notion that I had never before found myself in such inspiring company. It was more than the sheer intellect and eloquence of the conversation that impressed me. These men were among the most learned I had ever met. They seemed to understand every aspect of life, and each one had strong opinions based on sound reasoning. But above all, they were gentlemen, and gentlemen are a rare species in our modern dog-eat-dog world. I was honoured just to be included among them, and perhaps the highest honour of all was to be included as an equal and a friend.

CHAPTER 13

If man is to find greater happiness,
he must get back to nature and the natural ways.

The following afternoon after the time of rest and the passing of the heat of the day, I walked with Pahoran to the gathering place. We chatted about the things I'd learned in Yuwmah, and what I might write in my article on my return to the greater world. I told him of my struggle with the blank page, and how I had no idea where to begin. "Frankly, Pahoran," I bemoaned, "my experiences in Yuwmah are more than I'd expected, and perhaps more than I'm able to comprehend." He managed a polite chuckle.

"Unlike any story I've ever attempted, I have no obvious angle or theme," I mused. "After my efforts this morning, my notes are extensive, but they are without any sense of order or flow. I have a head full of thoughts and information, but I feel inadequate to transcribe them into fitting words and phrases." His smile was sincere but there was no reply as we walked on in silence.

At the gathering place we joined Mahonri and friends beneath the magnificent shade trees. Those seated around the table seemed to sense my confusion. Today there was no laughter—only quiet concern.

"What troubles your mind, my young friend?" asked Mahonri. "You look like my great-grandson when he tries to decide between honey and jam," he said gently.

My words came in a hesitant and hollow voice. "Today I intended to contact my team and instruct them regarding my return," I began, "although, I can't decide what to tell them. We expected that I would learn all I needed to know in just a few days, but each day brings new learning, and there appears to be no end to what I might discover if I stay longer."

"You know you are free to stay among us as long as you wish, Mr Saomes," said Mahonri. "What is the desire of your heart?"

I paused for a moment and tried to control the flood of thoughts. "As yet, I haven't been here for one of your five day weeks, so what might I miss if I leave today?" I asked.

"Tomorrow morning we practise the art of war. Mr Saomes. And in the afternoon we play at sports," said Pahoran.

"I would very much like to experience both activities," I decided. "I'd like to remain at least one more day. My other problem is my radio. After my efforts this morning, I've decided that it isn't strong enough to call out from here. I will need to rig an antenna to send a message."

"Perhaps we may be able to assist you, Mr Saomes. Do you know the frequency of your transmitter?" Mahonri asked.

"Yes I do," I replied, amazed that Mahonri knew of such things. "I remember it like my telephone number."

"Then there is something you must see," he replied. He stood and quietly beckoned me to follow. We left unobtrusively, following a path that took us among the buildings. After a short walk we came upon a grand palace stretching majestically before us.

"This building is our main centre of learning. It houses our library, a small hospital, and many other intellectual pursuits," said Mahonri. "It was once the palace of our kings. The spire to the left was erected to King Benyamin who was our last king and our first judge. He formally abdicated all authority over the people in favour of a system of judges so we might learn to choose our destiny for ourselves."

"He relinquished all dominion over his subjects and gave us back our freedom; though in time, the social system he established proved to be insufficient to maintain peace among such imperfect people. After his death we fell into fighting among ourselves. Groups holding opposing opinions rose up and shed blood to gain power and domination. Secret combinations developed and dark forces emerged. Without a guiding hand and clear regulation, we quickly descended into strife. It was an unpleasant time in our history, similar to the current situation in much of the world.

"That is the downside of having the right to choose, Mr Saomes. Unless the system we are bound by is perfectly fair, the weak may be dominated by the strong, the poor by the rich, and the innocent and uneducated by those who have greater knowledge and understanding. Superior knowledge is perhaps the most powerful weapon of all. This is why we must have charity to temper it. Otherwise, it may become a force for evil. When knowledge becomes power, it can overtake its possessor. Only charity and compassion ensure that knowledge is kept under control and used for good."

"If mankind will not rise above their base instincts, they will become driven by the quest for wealth and power. Selfishness and the lack of self-control are among the most destructive of all human weaknesses. Pride is the greatest stumbling block because those filled with pride are a danger to all and especially to themselves." Mahonri conveyed quietly.

"When we lose our sense of self-control and wallow in selfishness and become besotted by its accomplice, greed, we injure others and condemn ourselves. But when we are blinded by pride, we injure ourselves and condemn others unfairly. It is the way of the world, Mr Saomes. It has been so from the beginning and will continue until mankind can raise themselves above their animal desires and learn to control their passions appropriately for their own betterment."

"As long as man continues to be carnal and devilish they will continue to injure one another. If they are to rise above their senseless self-destruction, they must take control of their basic urges and aspire to a higher law and put aside petty jealousies, or they are doomed to remain subject to their own weakness."

Our conversation ceased at the entrance to the palace. Mahonri stopped short to instruct me.

"This is the most important of all our buildings because it contains things of great value to us. Good books are the source of knowledge, Mr Saomes. They are esteemed so highly that we adopt an attitude of the utmost humility as we enter. Therefore, we proceed in all sobriety and speak in whispers so as not to distract the concentration of others."

I nodded my compliance. We entered the outer court, which was indeed a marvel to behold. At that moment, I felt like a small child in pursuit of high adventure, searching for hidden treasure, or exploring the tombs and catacombs of an ancient and lost civilisation.

All around the courtyard were sculptures of bronze and marble, depicting Yuwmahn heroes. Standing in the centre was the imposing figure of a winged creature bearing down upon us from the heavens. The statue was a mythical looking creature with three horns above a giant eye, set between huge swirling wings upon a muscular body, with stout legs and a long flowing tail, all plated in gold leaf. The magnificent creature cast a massive shadow in the distinctive shape of an ancient Om symbol.

A grand arch spanned the entrance above us like a massive dome. Around the arch were hieroglyphic characters etched into the stone, similar to those found in the pyramids of Egypt. "This enormous signboard, Mahonri," I asked, pointing, "What does it signify?"

"This we call our Testament Plaque. There are similar inscriptions over each of the city entrances. Because each city is not governed by the same standards, we inscribe our specific values on a plaque so all who enter may know how to conduct themselves."

"The winged inscription in the centre is the Yuwmahn mark, a depiction of the golden statue, Mr Saomes. The three horns at the top of the eye symbolise past, present, and future, and the centrepiece is the 'all-seeing eye of God'. Its purpose here is to indicate that we are entering a holy place, that we are in His presence, that He sees all and knows all, and we are standing on sacred ground."

"The long flashing tail, the body with legs, and the wings symbolise the three attributes of Godliness, being omnipotence, omniscience, and omnipresence."

My blank look must have shown my lack of understanding. Mahonri quickly added, "All power, all knowledge, and a single presence whose influence can be felt everywhere. God is not ubiquitous, Mr Saomes.

He is not everywhere at once. His presence is felt everywhere because His influence is everywhere, but He is our Father—a man of flesh and bones like you and me. He is present in only one place, although as a God, He may freely move to anywhere He so chooses in the blink of an eye."

"And the other symbols?" I enquired. "What do they mean?"

"As with every community, the first line lists the personal aspects of conduct that the residents value and strive to uphold. These symbols are difficult to translate, Mr Saomes, but they are akin to 'mutual respect', 'courtesy', 'decency', and 'natural harmony'. The second line indicates the aspects of personal conduct we frown upon, which we deem unacceptable. The three emblems at the bottom loosely translate as 'no force', 'no excess', and 'no drugs'."

In stark contrast to the simplicity of their homes, the palace held every conceivable adornment: gold door handles, enormous murals and magnificent works of art covering the high walls, elaborately finished ceilings, and flowing marble staircases ascending to the floors above.

We passed rows of towering shelves laden with books. Dozens of people sat on padded chairs, oblivious to the world beyond their reading. Not a sound could be heard anywhere.

At the top of the central staircase we made our way along another corridor. Rooms and alcoves ran off to the right and left, each with small signs attached, like private offices. Mahonri indicated that their intellectuals occupied this level of the building: scientists and engineers, artists and musicians, health workers and planners. The plaques were in fact designations of speciality. The whole place felt much like a large university.

Midway along the passageway, Mahonri stopped and opened the massive door beside him, and bade me to enter. I walked into a small amphitheatre laid out like a classroom with rings of seats and desks inclined towards a central platform. Mahonri closed the door behind me and smiled broadly.

"This is one of our lecture theatres, Mr Saomes. We are alone at the moment, but let us move quickly as our time is short."

At the front of the room we stopped before a small cabinet. Mahonri moved to open the double doors and looked strangely at me.

"Are you prepared for what you might find here?" he asked.

"Lately, I am never quite ready for what comes next," I answered.

"Then prepare yourself for the unexpected, Mr Saomes," said Mahonri as he flung open the heavy cabinet.

"A radio!" I exclaimed aghast. "A two-way radio! I can't believe it."

"Yes, Mr Saomes! We have used this radio for many decades." His eyes widened as he continued, hands animated and expressive. "Often, at different times of the day, groups of people gather to listen to news broadcasts from near and far. We also receive a variety of informative and inspiring programmes in many languages. There is also a group who meets here to contact our people overseas. There are even members of our community in Australia, Mr Saomes. We own several properties there, just as we do in many countries around the globe," he smiled.

"Do you wish to send a message now, or would you rather tour our facilities first?"

"There's more?" I asked.

"Of course, Mr Saomes. We are an advanced civilisation here. There are still many things about us that you are not aware of. For example, we also have television! For decades there was no reception here, so we were limited to watching recorded documentaries brought back from the four corners of the world. But we have made significant advancements recently that I may disclose later."

"I wish to stress that we do not use these things for mindless entertainment or game playing, Mr Saomes. Such frivolity is perhaps the most subtly corrupting element of modern civilisation and would never be condoned here," he added.

He closed the heavy doors and turned to leave, pausing to point to a twisted cable that ran up the wall from behind the cabinet.

"There is a generator on the roof powered by gravitational force. We have learned to harness the force of gravity to generate electricity, Mr Saomes, so almost anything is possible, but the world at large is not ready for such an advancement."

As we left the auditorium, I wanted to delve into the detail of the gravity motor. I perceived that such an invention would have incredible and far-reaching ramifications; even to completely redesign the way the world operates, but Mahonri continued his commentary in another direction, so we moved on and my questions remained unanswered.

"The radio and televisions are relatively new projects that some of our people regard as a waste of time, but they tolerate them because others deem them to be of tremendous value. Of course, only time will tell."

"These devices put us in contact with the outside world and keep us abreast of news and current affairs. The Divine One's return is not far off, but certain things must come to pass first. Most of them are primed to happen soon. We are very close to the end of the world as we now know it, and our people are interested in monitoring the progress of events leading up to that day. We live in exciting times, Mr Saomes!"

I noticed the drop in Mahonri's voice as he made these comments. The second coming was obviously real to him, and for a moment I couldn't help but wonder what it would mean for me if it were actually true.

A short distance down the corridor, Mahonri paused again. "In here is our music collection, which also serves as a history of recording over the decades," he said, opening the door. Inside was a sizeable narrow room with rows of cabinets containing sound reels, records, cassettes, and compact discs. Around the walls were stations with players and headphones.

"Most of what you see here will eventually become outdated, Mr Saomes. In time these rooms will be a museum. Nothing is ever discarded in Yuwmah. No rubbish dumps, remember?" he smiled proudly.

"Was there no end to these people?" I asked myself under my breath.

Mahonri mentioned several sound lounges at the far end of the room where groups gathered to study and enjoy their music together. The next door revealed a classroom filled with musical instruments from around the world, where students could listen to and learn from their instructors.

Further down the corridor, we entered another theatre with walls covered with maps from every part of the globe. There was even a street map of Brisbane, on which I pointed out where I lived and worked. Other rooms and areas were dedicated to history, politics, and world religions. In a large conference room nearby, a lecture was in progress, conducted in German, concerning the current trends in the world financial system.

At the end of the corridor we climbed a short staircase to the highest level of the building. Mahonri opened the first door and my eyes bulged. Before me on a large circular platform was a giant telescope.

Three men stood to one side, comparing charts. All around the walls were brilliant illustrations of the planets and constellations.

"Among our people are some of the world's foremost academics, Mr Saomes. Members of our community have been at the cutting edge of scientific discovery for thousands of years, and part of almost every major advancement: from the telescope, to the telephone, to the silicon chip. Our people head teams, sponsor projects or participate in research committees. They live where they work, but return home now and then to visit family and friends. One of my own sons, a noted heart surgeon, will soon return from Europe for such a visit. It has been some years since we've seen him, so Misha and I are quite excited at the prospect of his return."

My head was spinning out of control as we walked further down the corridor. At the next door Mahonri stopped again, and I noticed his manner change as he lifted his withered fingers to the golden handles.

"The contents of this room are relatively new, and of particular importance, Mr Saomes. We refer to this place as our window to the world." Without further comment he twisted the heavy knobs and pushed the double doors inward. My eyes widened at the site before me and all at once I ceased to breathe. I found myself spluttering unrelated words in an unfamiliar voice. "How on earth? Not possible! This is ... unbelievable!"

I staggered a few steps into the large room, staring at the rows of people seated in front of computers and workstations, banks of switches, flashing lights, and electronic gadgetry. It reminded me of Mission Control at NASA.

"This can't be!" was all I could utter. Mahonri leaned in close to my ear and in reverent tones explained how they had used one of their aeronautical companies in Europe to build a privately owned telecommunications satellite to provide state of the art internet access.

"This facility gives us internet and communications capabilities which allow us to keep up with the ongoing political developments and technological advancements of the last days," he began. "We have teams of people manning these screens around the clock. My keyboard skills are probably not as proficient as yours, Mr Saomes, but can I help you to send an email to family or friends?"

"You have all of this Mahonri, yet ..." I shook my head as my mouth fell open again, but I could not articulate my thoughts beyond the guttural grunts coursing from my throat. Suddenly, and without warning, I felt my knees fold beneath me. Mahonri saw me falling and took my arm to steady me. After a moment, I found myself in an adjacent room where I sat in disbelief. A startled young woman came to help us, and after a few words she hurried off.

"Please lean back and relax, Mr Saomes. You appear to be overcome." Mahonri sat down beside me and placed a hand firmly on my shoulder. "Please rest and regain your strength. My granddaughter will bring us refreshments shortly."

I remember looking through dazed eyes and trying to open my mouth to speak, but I couldn't. It was all too much. I kept shaking my head, as though my brain had received too much information.

To this day I have little or no memory of what followed or how long I took to regain a sense of where I was. After a time, my thoughts began to take shape again but my mind was in such disarray. I wanted to ask Mahonri why they lived so primitively when clearly they could live any way they pleased—but I didn't have the strength.

Later, I walked on uncertain legs along the corridor towards the radio room. Dissociated thoughts rushed uncontrollably through my head, but at least I was conscious again. All at once I thoughtlessly blurted out, "Mahonri, how can you afford all of this equipment?" But as soon as the words left my lips I was embarrassed at the intrusive nature of such a question. I stopped to retract my outburst and apologise, but Mahonri's eyes met mine with a gentle gaze.

"What I tell you now is in complete secrecy, and I ask that it go no further than you and me, Mr Saomes. I wish to trust you with the full answer to your question."

Before I could nod, he continued. "Quite simply, we are all millionaires here. We have our own gold mine.

147

There are rich deposits not far from our city, which we have extracted over the centuries and moulded into the most beautiful ingots decorated with precious stones. In times past our travellers sold these in different places. Experts have classified and valued them as Mayan, Chinese, Sumerian, and even Egyptian artefacts. Our ancestry is coloured with all of these bloodlines so our people simply agreed and accepted payment!" he exclaimed with a broad grin.

"These days though, we look to our investments and business dealings. We have managed to amass more money than we could ever spend for many generations. We also buy and sell property around the world. We buy cheaply at the edge of a growing city and sell decades or even centuries later when prices have risen to millions. Our investment company has a diversified international portfolio which hedges against inflation and compensates for recessions and economic downturns."

"And because the world financial system was once tied to gold reserves, we are one of the richest communities on earth, especially on a per capita basis. There is almost nothing for sale that we could not buy if we desired, Mr Saomes—almost nothing at all. You can buy anything in this world with money, except the things we value the most, which cannot be bought because they cannot be sold."

"You see, here in Yuwmah, we dabble in the world of finance to enable our people to travel and participate in global affairs. But we are more concerned with seeking after those things that money cannot buy. They are far more valuable and desirable, and a truer measure of our personal and collective wealth. The attributes relating to a Godly character are out of reach of anyone who has not made an effort to develop them. For example, joy is the most priceless of all things. We cannot buy true joy with money. We cannot buy contentment or peace of mind. Neither can we buy self-respect or patience. But when we are truly content with ourselves and our lot, we can experience the greatest joy, even if we have no money at all."

"I'm sure it is a puzzle to you that we live so humbly when we could have anything our hearts desire, Mr Saomes. The answer to your conundrum lies in consciously choosing to reject a life that is cluttered, stressful, and fast-paced, as in the west—with televisions, computers, and electrical appliances invading your homes and your simple peace. Every choice has a consequence, remember? We don't wish to suffer the consequences of an unnatural life. The ultimate costs of living in such a way are not acceptable to us."

"The harnessing of electricity for example, was a major break-through for mankind. But in many ways man allowed its applications to change the world for the worse. We in Yuwmah see a definite role for electricity and many of the applications it makes possible, but we don't permit electrical devices to take over and rule our lives or ruin the beautiful world we were designed to inhabit."

"Nature's ways are self-regulating, Mr Saomes," continued Mahonri. The over-use of electrical devices has destroyed that self-regulation, and we have lost the simplicity and balance that once sustained us."

"If man is to find greater happiness, he must first find his proper place in the world and return to it. He must align himself with the natural variants and re-establish the circumstances that allow him to be at his physical and mental best. No electrical gadgetry or material possession can ever bring us lasting contentment. We find happiness in the simple things of life. Mankind must get back to nature and the natural ways, Mr Saomes."

"I find the greatest contentment here in my home surrounded by family and friends, and in living the life I was designed to live. Here I can feel totally at peace and remain unaffected by the pressures and problems of the greater world that electrical devices would unavoidably bring. As Misha often says, our home is like a piece of Heaven. Electricity, with all its gadgets and gizmos, would render it to be as complex and stressful as the developed world, which is not a heavenly environment for anyone!"

"But, if we desire to experience such advancements, we can come here to the library. Our people could have a laptop or tablet in every home if we chose to, but we seek to live in a more natural environment where such electronic intrusions are out of place."

"If we want to experience the full western lifestyle for a time, we can live anywhere we want, Mr Saomes!

Perhaps we might spend a season in the Mediterranean or in the heart of Los Angeles! I remember my first such excursion into the greater world. Misha and I accompanied several others who had been there before. In those days, we took some money from the repository and rode five days by donkey across the mountains to the river. Then we sailed for several days by boat to one of the larger cities, and from there we could go by ship to anywhere we chose."

"Of course, these days we usually travel by helicopter to the airport. We have purchased a charter service located close by on the coast. It has made our travel considerably faster and much simpler."

"But there are very few places I desire to visit again. I prefer to remain here to live in simplicity and peace, and enjoy the safety and harmony of the natural ways. There is too much conflict abroad, Mr Saomes. I find that life in the wider world has become far too complicated."

I could not have prepared myself for any of this. At the end of the tour, I made my excuses and went home to my dwelling without waiting for the evening meal. Frankly, I was a blithering mess. Today had been too much to take in and process.

I lay on my bunk for several hours and peered out the sky-window. Several times my tears welled up and poured down my cheeks. I had no idea why I was sobbing. I was not usually an emotional person. What was happening?

To look at these people, they appeared primitive and ignorant: mere peasants who lived and died with no understanding of anything. To speak with them was to learn they were more advanced and knowing than anyone I'd ever met. But to understand how they chose to live, and what they'd established here in the mountains and around the world, was more than I could comprehend.

CHAPTER 14

*We will one day be judged by the choices we make
within the most private recesses of our mind.*

Morning came too soon. I lay motionless, my thoughts confused and in disarray. I struggled to know what was real and worthwhile. I'd wrestled with unanswerable questions for most of the night without any form of clarity or understanding.

Nothing from the outside world made sense. All the sureties and certainties I'd ever believed seemed upside down. Every feeling of permanence—every solid aspect of my previous existence had been shattered or shot down in flames.

Eventually I got up and washed my face. In my muddled state I decided to send a message to the team requesting that they collect me immediately. My decision was based on the premise that I'd had more than enough of this place. I couldn't handle any more. I needed to withdraw and consider my options from a safe distance.

With each day here I felt more inferior and uncertain. In my mind, the stability and security of the world I once knew was daily collapsing into worthless rubble. I needed to return to it before it disintegrated completely. On a deeper level, lurking somewhere in the depths of my subconscious was the ever-growing notion that if I stayed here much longer, I might lose the desire to ever go back.

I changed my robe and set off to find Mahonri. Along the way I encountered small groups of men practising an interesting form of martial arts. They moved in ways that puzzled me. As a black belt in a similar discipline, I felt to find out more about their style and method. But first I had to send a message.

As I watched the men fighting with swords, spears, and a variety of unusual weapons, I decided they were incredibly skilled and definitely not playing! I spotted Mahonri with a few men beneath the shade trees. They were gathered in a loose circle, evidently engaged in serious business. Mahonri appeared to be their instructor. He was standing between two of them who were younger than myself. They watched intently as he demonstrated a series of moves. I approached within his field of vision, but his full attention remained with his charges.

I could hear Mahonri speaking to them sternly in their own language. Without warning he jumped back with incredible stealth and the two combatants faced each other with real intent. They spun and swung and leapt about, but neither made contact with the other. Then Mahonri was back between them with a few encouraging words and an unmistakable look of satisfaction. After his comments he stepped away, signalling them to continue. It was only now that we made eye contact and he moved to my side wearing his usual broad smile.

"Good morning, Mr Saomes. Shall we walk a little? Isn't it a glorious morning?"

Mahonri headed off through the groups of sparring warriors towards a vacant area close by, and I followed close behind.

"Did you sleep well, Mr Saomes?" he asked in a gentle tone. Amid my confusion I shook my head.

"Mahonri, in all honesty, I have never felt more confused in my life."

Mahonri stopped and turned to face me. "What troubles you, my young friend?" he enquired.

"I can't begin to explain, but I think you know. You have more insight than anyone I've ever met. Do you understand my current predicament, Mahonri? Do you see what keeps me from sleeping?"

"Yes, I believe I do," he began. "I perceive that yours is a struggle that every man and woman must face at some stage of their life. It is all the harder for you because you must decide your future path by choosing between something acceptable and familiar, and something that is potentially better but largely unknown—between the memories of your past and the realities of your present. Such choices are difficult for anyone."

The aged man reached out a gentle hand and placed it on my shoulder. "Sometimes in life we reach a situation where we must choose between two desirable possibilities," he began. "What makes the decision more difficult is the circumstance where we cannot have one without sacrificing the other. When we cannot have both at the same time, we have to decide which option we want most, and face the reality that the other is gone, perhaps forever. This is often the hardest of all choices to truly commit to."

I struggled to grasp his meaning, and wanted to tell him so—but he continued before I could speak.

"If we are to have the best that life can give, and to live at the pinnacle of human existence, this is a path we must come to know well. Most people settle for mediocrity because such decisions are too hard. Often they cannot give up one thing to fully embrace another, even though they believe the other is potentially the better choice. This becomes a test of character rather than an exercise of simple choosing."

I was beginning to grasp the full impact of his comments and managed to interject before he could say more.

"Mahonri, I have truly come to appreciate your city and your ways. I am very much at home here too, but my future is so clear if I return. Here it is so uncertain, yet so very desirable."

"But that is not all that troubles you, my young friend," Mahonri responded. "There are deeper issues here that must be dealt with or they will eventually consume you and leave you lost forever. Pride is a terrible stumbling block to personal growth and progress, Mr Saomes. To conquer pride and embrace humility is not a simple process, but it is always the better choice. You know well enough that it's a certain kind of fool who craves the sound of his own name."

"I knew you would understand," I said. "In the outside world I am well-known and respected, which is something I value tremendously. Is this only pride that I can cast off, or is it part of who I am? I feel a sense of duty to my readers and my employer to return and continue my work there. Aren't these things important too?"

Mahonri's answer was resolute. "But what will it profit a man if he gains the recognition of the whole world but loses his own soul? There is very little a man can do in this life that really matters. Perhaps the greatest work we ever do will be done within the four walls of our own home, which few will ever know."

"We will one day be judged, Mr Saomes. Of this we can be certain. The criteria for that judgement are not clear, but perhaps even more than the sum total of our life's work, we will be judged on the choices we make within the most private recesses of our mind."

"We came into this life to learn to choose good over evil, and to fight for the right to do so. It is my humble opinion that our choices will exalt us or condemn us.

Ultimately, we must learn to choose for ourselves and be prepared to account for our choices to a higher power."

"Every choice we make has an inescapable consequence, my young friend. When we choose to do one thing, there is often a myriad of outcomes that automatically follow. In our mind we must learn to see past the original choice and focus on what will change as a result, because it is the consequences of our choices that we live with each day thereafter. By this manner of choosing we learn to become the master of our own destiny rather than the victim of our follies. To become the master of our destiny is to obtain the crowning glory of mortality—the greatest achievement this life can bring, and the highest state of existence known to man."

By early afternoon I sat beside the wheel-tracks where the plane had left me a few days earlier. I was dressed in a Yuwmahn robe and poncho, a funny three-sided hat, and brightly coloured bandanna—cheeks bristling with the rough beard on my suntanned face. My gaze fell to the soft shoes. I remembered the silence as I walked across the hard earthen road out of the city by the south gate.

Behind me stood a group of people I'd come to know more intimately than my closest friends. A few short days ago they had welcomed me into their world. Now they'd come to bid me farewell.

At the time of my arrival I valued my life above anything I might find here. But now I was not so sure.

Perhaps to discover the higher purposes of life we must first lose ourselves in the service of others as the Yuwmahns had taught me.

As I sat motionless on my pack, I recalled the thought that any story I might find here would be a small consolation to the sparing of my miserable self. But as I weighed the importance of what I'd discovered, surely the sacrifice of a single life was a small price to pay when compared to the tremendous benefits the world might gain from such ancient wisdom. Through the pages of history, thousands of men such as I had freely given their lives for lesser causes.

In the distance I heard the noise of the plane and turned to watch as it approached. Even at this late stage I was contemplating the idea of ending my old life to embrace a new one. All I had to do was walk back into the forest and leave my earthly troubles behind. I knew the plane was low enough for those on board to see me, though I was unaware of the conversation unfolding in the cockpit—a conversation that God alone may have directed.

"I'm not even sure this is the right valley. They all look the same at this altitude, and the GPS keeps changing its mind. Let's try further up."

"Hey! Is that him down there?"

"Nah ... just another one of those dumb Indians."

CHAPTER 15

Examine your life. Give thought to every aspect.
Find ways to make every moment better.

There was I, and what a sight I was. I sat looking skyward at the fading connection to my past existence. Peering through a thick haze of uncertainty I felt smothered—unable to draw breath. Distorted images flashed through my mind like mirages in the heat of a summer sun.

For a time I sat there—all alone. Perhaps I had died and was now waiting in purgatory for someone to lead me to the next phase of my existence. As I stared blankly into space, the last few days of my life flashed through my head as a vast panoramic vision, like a scroll unrolling out of heaven, or was it out of hell? I saw with my inner eye a condensed flashback, like a detailed record inscribed in the annals of my personal history by the angels who secretly watch over me.

Off in the distance I glimpsed my editor's secretary waving me off and wishing me well. Hours of ocean passed beneath me, and a thousand nameless islands bobbing like corks in the rolling sea. I beheld the awesome ranges of the Andes Mountains rising out of the waters like the tail of a mythical serpent. I blinked and squinted but the vision continued. I saw myself clambering into the tiny Cessna, which carried me beyond the edge of civilisation, landing in a field of lush grass and brilliant wildflowers. And there in the distance was the group of curious Indians coming towards me.

With each image came a blur of memories, affecting my mind so powerfully that I could barely bring myself to revisit them. In the final scene on my scroll of life, I saw myself fleeing the walled city and the people I'd come to love and admire. I saw myself walking to the spot where I now sat. The sound of the humming motors stayed with me as the plane flew out of sight into the afternoon sun.

I remember waving, but they didn't acknowledge me, as if I'd blended into the rocks and trees and earth like a native. At that very moment, somewhere deep inside my soul I felt a changing, as though a tiny hand was moving back and forth, silently erasing all record of my previous existence in the greater world.

As I looked around me, I knew I was alive. Beyond that basic fact there was little else I was sure of. Then I heard a noise, a hollow voice cutting through the haze that engulfed me—the sound of my own name—calling me forth, as if from the grave, and back into mortality.

"Mr Saomes ... Mr Saomes. It would seem that God has decreed that you remain among us. It is late. We must return to the city before nightfall."

I looked around and found myself standing in the midst of strangers, yet they were familiar, like family. Surely I was not one of these people? They looked so alien and different to my perception of myself. At that moment, I knew where I was, yet I felt lost and far from home. This was not my land or my country. Most of all, I wondered why I was still here. I felt like a frightened bird, fallen from its nest into a foreign and foreboding world I could barely recognise.

As the crowd around me began to disperse, I moved along with them, my legs functioning independently of my mind, carrying me away without my permission. How dare they!

Still, who could argue in such a situation? We walked briskly into the twilight as the sun sank behind the snow-capped peaks. When our party reached the edge of the cornfields, I could see the city ahead. A solitary lantern lit the south gate, but the expanse of the wall faded into darkness. As we approached, I heard the bell toll three times. It was a comforting ring yet it implied something I was not prepared for. It signalled that a group of villagers were safe home from the wilderness and all was well. The bells bore audible witness that I was no longer a stranger but one of their own, as though I'd forfeited my old identity and assumed a new one.

Inside the gate Mahonri asked gently, "Would you like to eat, Mr Saomes, or would you rather go to your home and sleep?"

My reply echoed in my ears as if I'd spoken my first words. "Home—thank you."

Inside my familiar dwelling I stretched out and lay motionless on the bed, looking up at the low clouds as if I were trapped in a dream. The next thing I knew, I was back in the valley, waving my arms as the aircraft passed almost overhead. But it did not circle. It did not stop. It just kept going. Still waving, I watched it grow smaller in the pale sky until it was gone, and I was alone.

Then came a distant voice calling my name. "Mr Saomes ... Mr Saomes." I woke in fright and sat up gasping great gulps of breath. My arms were thrashing about as if fighting an unseen foe. With eyes wide, my face was tight and ghostly white. I could feel my heart pounding in my chest and the rush of blood pulsing through my head. Falling back on the bunk I panted deeply, my whole body lathered in a cold sweat.

What followed next was the strangest sensation. I blinked and rubbed my eyes. Something was touching my face. I reached out to find no one. After a moment, I realised that rain was falling through the sky-window, which closed with a bump as I released the cord beside my bed. Nearby, similar bumps rang out in the night.

I wiped icy droplets from my sprinkled face with the palms of my hands, and for the first time in hours I felt alive.

So here was I, and what a sight I was. Over these past few days I'd come to realise that the high-tech, fast-paced world I'd been part of for the past forty years was less than its boast. Yuwmah was without the problems plaguing the developed world. The people here were free, and because of a strange twist of fate I was now considered one of them.

Was any of this real? Could such a place be as wonderful as I'd come to believe? Were the people as advanced and Godly as they appeared? Did they really have all the answers? Did their way of life here in the mountains really represent the best way for man to live?

Without reason I began to cry, shamelessly sobbing, torrents of emotion pouring down my cheeks like the aftermath of a tropical storm. As the tears flooded from my eyes, all the pent-up frustrations magically washed away, leaving me more stable than I'd been for some time. Perhaps I was in shock, or maybe I was coming out of it. Either way, I felt much better when the weeping was over. 'A time to laugh and a time to cry,' I thought to myself. Yes, it was all happening here!

As the night deepened, I struggled with the realities of my plight. Reason suggested two options. I could use the facilities in the library to reschedule the plane for my departure, or disappear from the known world and stay here indefinitely. Morning came unannounced before I reached a decision. I answered a knock at the door to find Mahonri and his lovely wife Misha holding a tray containing my breakfast.

"Good morning, Mr Saomes. How are you feeling this morning?" Misha asked cheerfully.

"I cannot begin to tell you, Misha, but please come in," I replied. We sat around the wooden table in silence. I sensed they were waiting for me to begin the conversation, but I was without words.

"Did you sleep, Mr Saomes?" Mahonri ventured.

"I guess I must have, but it was a very long night," I muttered.

"Please try to eat something," said Misha. "You must eat to keep up your strength."

I thanked her for her kindness but I was not hungry. I toyed with the cereal and nibbled on a few grains as we sat surveying each other's faces. Finally, Mahonri looked deep into my eyes and asked politely, "Mr Saomes, what is in your heart?"

I tried to answer but there was too much to say. Mahonri placed his hand on my shoulder and spoke in a gentle, fatherly way, as if to a troubled child.

"May I offer some suggestions?" came his knowing request. "Your present state of mind concerns me. Perhaps I might provide some advice and direction."

I found myself nodding and opening my senses to any comments this 'man among men' might extend.

"Anyone who has lost sight of their future must rise above the cloud of confusion that darkens their imagination. To do this, you must start from within. You must do what is necessary to find peace in your heart and solace for your soul, and regain a sense of balance. You must shake off the seeds of doubt that cling to the troubled mind and find your true self, and unmask your deepest desires, or you will remain lost forever."

"These are fine words," I replied. "But how do I give them meaning?"

"Step by step, my friend! Step by step!" was his smiling reply.

"Mr Saomes, you are confused. You don't have the answers you seek because you have not yet asked the most important questions. Permit me to provide a question that may lead to the answers you are struggling to find. *What will bring you the greatest happiness?*"

After a moment he continued. "Do not settle for simple fun or empty distraction like a child at an amusement park. Look deeper for the source of true and lasting joy that will warm your soul, both now and forever. I suggest that this is your greatest goal, for it is the ultimate goal of every one of us. The answer to this question encapsulates that 'secret something' that all mankind seeks to know. Indeed, to find this answer is the very purpose of life and the greatest challenge of all."

"Many find temporary substitutes for real happiness. The closest word in your language is 'fun'. Because they fail to look beyond the 'here and now' they seek immediate gratification and sell themselves short. Fun is a poor substitute for true happiness because it is shallow and does not last longer than a moment, but it is all that some can manage."

"You, Mr Saomes, must lift your gaze from the patch of earth in front of your feet. Plan not for your next footstep; first consider your options and find a direction for that step. Too often people plod onward to nowhere because they lack direction. And because they see only their next footstep, they miss the scenery along the way. Extend your field of vision and look around, Mr Saomes. Find the things that matter most: the things that will make a real difference. Seek for that which gives your life a sense of purpose and the opportunity for achievement and enduring joy.

"Examine your life. Give thought to every aspect. Find ways to make every moment better. Even with the good things that bring you a measure of happiness, seek out the more excellent way. And remember—even small things can steadily pull us down. Cease to tolerate that which gnaws away at you. Such can be replaced with new and different ways. Every aspect of your situation can be improved if you try. Constant growth and improvement are the hallmarks of a good and happy life, Mr Saomes."

"And as part of your personal reflection, might I add a further challenge. Each of us must formulate and adopt what we in Yuwmah call our 'rules for life'. You must be clear about the things you will accept as appropriate, and even more determined about that which is not appropriate. Then you must set yourself a few rules to live by and vow never to break them. 'I will never take that which does not belong to me' for example. 'I will always tell the whole truth and not cover my sins, be they sins of commission or sins of omission'—the things I did and shouldn't have, or the things I should have done but didn't."

"When we define our 'rules for life', we define who we are and what we stand for. By the limits we set for ourselves, we can gauge our progress. The measure of a good man is an ongoing process, Mr Saomes. Every day we refine ourselves by re-defining ourselves—little by little. We must be driven by a staunch determination to do better. But first we must lay our foundations to build from."

"A set of rules by which we govern ourselves is the place to start. The key to this process is the concept that 'the weight of our sincerity is measured by the minimum standards we allow ourselves to accept'. If we tolerate injustice or turn a blind eye to wrong-doing, or accept any degree of foolishness; if we allow ourselves to be less than we could be; if we indulge our animal passions when we should do better and aim higher—we are not acting in our own best interests. The happiness that comes from self-mastery is our goal, which comes to us step by step, year by year—one decision at a time."

"In the greater world, goal setting is a process people use to work towards a place or condition they want to reach. Quite simply, to reach that place or condition, our first and most important exercise is to picture the kind of person we might become if we controlled ourselves as we know we should. We then set about planning our steps to make that journey possible and fix our vision towards that goal through the seasons of our life."

"If we see ourselves as healthy, vibrant centenarians, we need to decide in our youth to be active and eat nutritious food, and not take harmful substances that destroy our longevity. In other words, we decide the consequences we wish to create and set out to discern the actions that create them. We should always look at the consequences of every action first and foremost, rather than the action alone!"

"Over the time you have dwelt among us, Mr Saomes, your eyes have been opened. You now see beyond the words. You have come to realise the tragic nature of the ways of the modern world and to see the futility of many of the traditions and habits of your forefathers. You've opened your mind and your heart to glimpse a better and more excellent way. Like the boy who becomes a man, you must now find that way for yourself and set your own rules to live by and pursue your own path to happiness."

I grasped his message plainly, but I felt inadequate to make the changes that would release my better self. "I hear the wisdom of your words, Mahonri, but how do I act upon them?" I sobbed. "How will I find such answers when I can barely understand the questions?"

"Stay with us. Live among us. Learn from us," Mahonri urged. "If we are to find answers, there is no better place or time to look than 'here and now'. God will bestow greater light and knowledge upon all who are prepared to receive it. You must prepare yourself. You must begin anew with the curiosity and humility of a child. Cast aside the foolish habits that weigh you down and consider the greater possibilities. Commence today, Mr Saomes. Commence today!"

CHAPTER 16

If everyone tried to make the world a better place ...
if each of us plays our part, all the problems
of modern society could be cured.

Mahonri sat back and placed an affectionate hand on my shoulder before continuing his commentary. "Until you know who you are and what you stand for, Mr Saomes, you will struggle to make better decisions and find the greatest happiness—for how can anyone find something when they know not what it looks like? I perceive that much of your confusion comes from not knowing yourself as well as you might."

"To truly come to know ourselves we must ask a few simple questions. What do I really want from life? What do I value and what is unacceptable? What aspects of my world are the most important to me, and which are pointless distractions or manifestations of selfish laziness? In finding such answers we begin to realise what our soul yearns for."

"Once we understand ourselves, we know immediately how to think and act to our greatest advantage, because most of the important decisions are already made. When we haven't found answers to such questions, our treasure remains elusive because we don't know what we're looking for."

"To see ourselves as we are, we must first peel back the layers of our lives and examine the core of our being. Happiness comes by steady steps towards a better situation. We can strive to satisfy the shallower aspects of our being, but there is limited joy to be found in doing so. Only when we appease the very heart are we deeply satisfied and content. This is real happiness, Mr Saomes—not one of the fake fads of the wanton world!"

"This is where you must begin. You would be wise to take stock of your current situation. Once we understand who we are and truly know our own mind, the next question is, 'From here—where to?' In other words, 'What changes would you like to make', or 'Who do you want to be'?"

"If we asked those in the west what they wanted most, they would probably choose a bigger home, a nicer car, or more money in the bank. Such things to us here in Yuwmah have little meaning. But most people in the west have those things already, so they just want more."

"The wiser thought is to know how much is enough. Only when we're grateful for what we have are we able to appreciate the bigger and better, and only when we know how much is enough can we be completely content."

After a thoughtful silence I turned to the ageing man before me. "What keeps you going Mahonri? Where do you find your passion for life and such a strong sense of purpose?"

His answer came slowly and with real intent, and I shall never forget each laboured word. "As I consider my own mortality, I find myself challenged with the same questions that face everyone who has ever lived, especially the age-old question of, 'Why are we here?' And how do we attach a purpose to our life knowing full well that one day we will be old and fade away?"

"When I had young children, there was a reason to go on. I felt a sense of purpose and urgency each day because my children depended on my care and support. But now that I am almost without responsibility for anyone, my time is my own, and I must find ways to fill it, just like you, Mr Saomes."

"As I struggle with the concept of living a purposeful life, I look around at others and consider their situations. The only two alternatives I see are as old as life itself: to live a life of self-indulgence where everything is about 'me', or to pursue a life dedicated to the service of others. One option embraces the idea of having as much fun as we can; to 'eat, drink, and be merry, for tomorrow we shall die'. The other suggests losing one's self in the service of our fellow man, to serve a higher and more noble purpose, and to open ourselves to the possibility of helping others who may one day return the favour. If we all commit ourselves to serving one another—what a wonderful world we can create and what a marvellous life we might live."

"I am convinced that a life of self-indulgence, grasping for every possible moment of fun and frolic that we stumble across, is a shallow existence of minimal consequence. There is no planning for a purposeful or vibrant future. To me, to spend one's life aimlessly fighting over the crumbs that fall from other men's tables, rather than making the effort to plan a feast and set a table of our own design, is a poor alternative. The level of joy available to us when we elevate our vision and seek to serve one another and aim for the higher purposes of life is far more rewarding and fulfilling."

"A life of service has appeal on a number of levels, Mr Saomes. I still remember my grandfather's teachings. First, it gives us a sense of purpose and a reason to get out of bed each morning. Secondly, it provides a challenge that leads to a deep sense of accomplishment and fulfilment as we succeed. Thirdly, it provides us with a social framework of associates and friends, and activities that keep life interesting. Service to others enables us to break new ground, giving us opportunities to learn and grow. We derive immense satisfaction as we see good things come from our efforts. And finally, it is said that service brings us closer to God."

"Of course, we can also focus on self-improvement and challenge ourselves to be better. This is a splendid use of our time and energies. But application is the key. Ultimately, we need to improve and refine ourselves so we can better serve others rather than ourselves."

"A life characterised by service is therefore the only option I consider worthwhile. By its very nature it is rewarding because I also believe in karma. There seems to be an unwritten law in the universe that stipulates that the more we give, the more we receive in return."

"Most of all, helping others who are less fortunate than myself makes me feel blessed every day. Such a labour makes me want to give back even more as I learn to appreciate all that I have. My life is full and filled with meaning and purpose. I feel rich, Mr Saomes. Very rich indeed."

"It's not hard to do something for someone to brighten their day. The hardest part is finding the motivation. In doing so, you benefit your own life immeasurably. A word of warning though, some people do things for others with the expectation of getting something in return. Then they become disappointed when their desired reward doesn't appear. It would be better for such people to work towards their own ends. Only when we give unselfishly and expect nothing in return, do we begin to be a true servant of all, and only then can we be blessed from on high."

"If everyone tried to make the world a better place, can you see the possibilities? Can you see the potential of everyone doing some small thing to help others along their way? I have come to believe that if each of us plays our part, all the problems of modern society could be cured!"

The following evening, Mahonri pulled me aside from the usual crowd and ushered me to a quiet spot some distance from the food servery. "How are you, my young friend?" he asked with a sense of deep concern.

"I scarcely know where to start," came my tentative reply, "but I felt better after our talk yesterday. First and foremost, I'm pleased to be alive. The rest is quite scrambled, but at least I have my feet on the ground and I have a good friend who watches over me," I smiled.

He grinned broadly in obvious delight and ran his arm around my shoulder. "You'll be okay," Mahonri replied. "Like every moment of uncertainty and despair, yours too shall pass. In time you will find a greater sense of balance and direction, and your future will become clear once again."

Time unfolded in Yuwmah in a magical way. I worked and played, danced and laughed, and discussed the things of God, of man, and the universe. I read and studied, and practised the art of war. I also deliberated upon the greatest of all questions. Over time, I learned about the world around me and the person within, and especially of the character I might one-day become.

With each passing day I was feeling renewed: transformed into a better person. My life became rich and delightful, and happiness filled my soul. Eventually, I felt as though I'd found that special secret that people the world over were seeking but could not find—that sacred elixir of life, that precious essence of humanity.

Through the weeks and months, Yuwmah had become my home and my fortress. I was among friends, safe and content. I was also on a personal journey to become Yuwmahn, a person of noble existence and a higher call, of greater substance and Godly character. Through my opened eyes I'd glimpsed the pinnacle of human potential. In short, I was becoming a better being—a Yuwmahn being.

CHAPTER 17

*Our beautiful world is degenerating at a horrific pace
and groaning under the weight of
unbridled destruction.*

The higher peaks of the nearby mountains were now capped with snow, and a chilling winter wind blew from their direction. As the seasons changed around me in glorious wonder, I noted that my person was thinner and more athletic than I'd been in twenty years. I felt young and vibrant and very much alive.

Many Yuwmahns wore an undergarment like long johns beneath their robe and poncho, yet we continued to meet in the gathering place as always. Tubs of glowing charcoal were placed around the tables to provide warmth.

Despite the brisk climate, we were not uncomfortable. Our bodies seemed to adapt—fortified against the elements by our nutritious diet and healthy lifestyle. I was not accustomed to such cold, but my life continued much as usual.

One afternoon I found myself sitting with a group of friends in the gathering place. Toosa and his wife had returned the previous night from their first trip around the world. A large crowd gathered to hear their remarks. I anticipated a long drawn-out travelogue of humorous and memorable happenings, with perhaps a few nail-biting adventures along the way. To my amazement, the tone of their commentary was entirely different. I translated their comments as follows:

"It is such a relief to be home at last! Over the past five hundred days we have toured the world in pursuit of learning and knowledge. My dear wife and I studied extensively before we departed, but nothing could have prepared us for what we found. Sadly, we report that our beautiful world is degenerating at an alarming pace and groaning under the weight of unbridled destruction."

"When we departed, we had an expectation of how things might be—but everything was far worse than imagined. Population control continues to be the most pressing concern, with terrible consequences. Religious and political wars, and viral outbreaks have done much to reduce numbers around the globe, especially in the fourth world, with horrific outcomes."

"To the members of the Circle of Philemon here present, we wish to report that your concerns regarding the measures initiated to limit global population are accurate and well justified. The AIDS virus has claimed millions, particularly in the underdeveloped countries, leaving many African villages populated by small children and a few elderly. More recently, the Ebola virus has had a similar effect. No doubt those who engineered and released those diabolical weapons are well pleased with their efforts."

"The 'one child' policy in China, of grave concern to many, has been less effective than was hoped. It would seem that the Asian bird flu and the droughts and inclement weather delivered by the International Weather Machine are proving far more effective. As expected, the tsunamis, extreme storms and droughts, especially around the equatorial belt have worsened over the past decade, and we may yet feel the effects here in our sheltered valley."

"It is probable that those who try to manipulate the global weather patterns with their solar reflection satellites and the charging of the ionosphere did not anticipate the flow-on effects, or the degree to which their tinkering would indirectly influence their own condition. Havoc has been felt in many nations around the world because of their malicious meddling."

"I should also report that population control efforts are now being tied directly to agriculture. Crops are systematically destroyed for political advantage as well as population reduction. As expected, Russia has been the worst hit, with drier summers and harsher winters. Starvation has claimed many, but the resulting political unrest brings the most propitious victory to her enemies. It appears that the Russian programme is close to its end because there is little left to gain. The anticipated invasion and take-over by foreign interests and capitalist magnates is almost complete."

"The world financial markets are less predictable. The World Bank is struggling, and every country will soon fall into endless recession if the world's mega-rich continue on their current course. As most of you know, we have reached the point where many individuals and companies are richer than whole countries. The wholesale buying and selling of currencies is having a terrible effect on exchange rates. Those who possess large sums of a particular currency are now in a position to bankrupt nations."

"As a result, political agendas are being manipulated or controlled by individual interests while governments struggle to avoid financial catastrophe. The incessant squabbling among the world's megalomaniacs is out of control, and the ordinary citizens around the globe are daily feeling the brunt of their follies."

"In the recent past when syndicates controlled the financial markets, there was a semblance of order. But now that the super-rich have become so powerful in their own right, and financial markets are more open and unprotected, and greed has escalated to frightening levels. If some control is not reinstated soon, the whole financial system will collapse and there will be tremendous suffering, especially among the peasantry."

"Also, many of the world's most tranquil and beautiful havens are being transformed into capitalist playgrounds. These dens of iniquity cater to the wealthy and a whole spectrum of inconsequential 'celebrities', glorified for their subtly corrupting and divisive contributions."

"Buildings are appearing like scars on the world's most pristine landscapes, with wilful destruction of some of the most important and valuable habitats. Governments turn a blind eye to developers that destroy the natural beauty and devastate the local way of life— all in the name of progress and economic advantage. The quest for the mighty dollar is ripe the world over, as is the cold-heartedness that accompanies such ambitious and unconscionable endeavours. Capitalism, as we well know, brings out the worst of human nature."

"The ghettos in many of the bigger cities are growing ever more violent, to such a degree that police no longer patrol many areas. The drug lords reign, and crime continues to proliferate out of control. The people live in fear, trapped by generations of poverty and tradition, and feelings of utter hopelessness."

"I should add that due to the growing global unrest among the people, the One World Government and associated United Nations programmes are struggling to establish a firm foothold. As previously noted, the proposed system for global control is being resisted by the citizens of almost every country at a level not foreseen by its designers."

"Almost every sinister effort to engineer a global outcome has been challenged. The protest is not coming from governments, because most are prepared to sacrifice the independence and self-determination of their populations for a place of prestige on the world stage. The real challengers are the ordinary folk who love their homeland, who are prepared to die to defend their values and their traditional way of life. Previously peaceable individuals are banding together to stand against their oppressors. Tradition, family ties, and religious beliefs, are proving to be far stronger than originally anticipated."

"Pollution is worse now than ever, but less obvious. Civic efforts have cleaned up local degradations, but the elevated levels of fumes and poisonous gases in the atmosphere remain largely unattended. These gases retain heat and create the greenhouse effect, melting the polar caps and causing the oceans to rise. Consequently, many low-lying islands are disappearing. Global warming has been allowed to escalate for financial gain and is now evident everywhere."

"Deforestation continues to be the main cause, with enormous tracts of forest being logged and cleared daily. Due to the lack of trees and grasslands, an insufficient amount of carbon dioxide is being recycled into breathable air, and carbon is not being captured and turned back into vegetation from whence it came. Yet the nations of the world continue to hold meetings to agree on decreasing emissions, when they should focus on neutralising their emissions through reaforestation. It's such a simple process to restore the delicate balance. Of course, there is much profit to be made from such a catastrophe."

"The greatest benefit of the ongoing threat of global warming to the western nations is the perceived need to develop renewable energies. The turning away from fossil fuels in favour of cleaner industries is a direct attempt to neutralise the leverage of the oil-rich Arab nations. Removing the demand for oil from the Middle East would decrease earning capacity and nullify their virtual monopoly. Limited demand for oil will render them penniless and powerless, which appears to be the main outcome the West conspires to achieve."

"Education around the world has been replaced by blatant indoctrination, and logic has given way to unbridled emotional debate. Widespread and systematic de-sensitisation programmes have blurred the truth to such a degree that most legal documents can now be construed to mean almost anything. Wills and treaties are being contested as never before, and many are suing others for preposterous reasons."

"Private schools are funded heavily by governments to ensure their adherence to a national curriculum. This ensures that global social engineering and socialist indoctrination has greater penetration among the masses."

"The right of the individual to self-determination is all but gone and democracy has been trampled by secret combinations of socialist forces. International covenants are secretly entered into by complicit governments in defiance of the democratic process, especially among the more powerful nations."

"On a wider scope, the humanists have systematically worked their way into most of the highest and lowest places imaginable. The humanist agenda is unfolding at a frightening pace. Indeed, the humanists themselves have declared this to be the 'century of humanism'. Their fiendish fingers are everywhere, manipulating social policy globally."

"Any reference to God or prayer will soon be removed from schools and government institutions. Religions will be brought into disrepute, and religious practices and beliefs will be openly condemned. In their place we are witnessing an upsurge in overstated 'scientific certainty' as the basis of all belief."

"We are also seeing the rise and acceptance of minorities such as the gay communities, the transgender movement and so forth. While such have been despised for thousands of years and labelled as misfits, there is an enormous global push by the humanists for greater tolerance, to force acceptance of all manner of perverse characters as mainstream citizens. To further this effort, gay rights campaigners are given every opportunity by the media to further their cause, and being gay or supporting the gay movement has become the latest social imperative. Every voice of opposition is decried by the same media so that opponents are effectively silenced because they are not given a public voice to express their concerns."

"Over the past few years, these and other humanist policies and ideals have been thrust upon the masses with unrelenting effort. There has been a considerable push by the feminist lobby for equal numbers of women in previously male dominated areas, even though many believe women are generally less suited to such positions."

"We note for example that governments of several countries have encouraged women into combat roles in their armed forces for the first time in history. Police services are similarly served with a growing number of women assigned to the front lines. The humanists see this as a victory because they regard such changes as creating a more equal society; yet to many, it is a sad day when their precious women are placed in hostile, dangerous, and brutal situations they are not physically strong enough to deal with."

"The traditional trouble spots around the globe continue as they have for centuries. On the surface their leaders talk of peace, but underneath they work towards their own advantage and the destruction or enslavement of their traditional enemies. Many of these conflicts go back thousands of years and will only escalate as time passes because neither side wish to negotiate."

"Religious wars are also on the increase, with the more zealous Muslims rising up against the moderates of their own faith in the name of their God. Those who take a moderate approach have been accepted and encouraged by the west, yet they are called traitors by the more devout and are being put to death by the thousands because of their reluctance to uphold the scriptural fundamentals of their doctrine."

"Millions of Muslims are being slaughtered because they choose not to take the hard line as expressed in their holy book. The traditional Christian world has been slow to act, preferring instead to antagonise the situation and prolong the killing, so that the influence and spread of Islam might be lessened in the world.

"The Muslim holy book, the Koran, calls for the true believers to kill and terrorise Christians wherever they find them. In fact, it teaches plainly that all non-believers should be beheaded or killed. Therefore, there is much concern in the devout Muslim world that their religion has become diluted. Considerable debate continues about how literally they should interpret their scriptures in the modern world. Those who take the more literal approach have been labelled 'extremists' when really they are the more faithful."

"Recent 'fatwas'; doctrinal interpretations espoused by Mufti leaders on both sides; have included a 'call to arms' indicating that fighting will only escalate. As the nations of the world align, either 'for' or 'against', many countries have proposed to exterminate the hardliners."

"The threat of terror attacks and bloodshed around the world is new to many countries, with the people reeling at the prospect of beheadings, open violence, and retaliations on their streets. In recent times the Muslim uprising has become the most pressing global concern, bringing terrorism and fear into the lives of innocent and peace-loving people the world over."

"In short my friends, our planet cannot long continue in its current mode. There are presently more displaced persons around the world than ever before in history: even more than after the great wars. May the people cry out with a single voice against the destruction of our earthly home. May those who propose to be the custodians of this planet act with urgency to avert the imminent and ongoing destruction, and may the Divine One return soon to save us from deepening suffering. This concludes our report."

I was gob-smacked! I couldn't grasp the full significance of all that was said, but I understood enough to realise the essence of his message. My personal take was along the lines of, 'the world is in a mess and everyone knows it, but most people feel powerless to make a difference'.

I was well aware of the problems, but I felt like an innocent bystander, ill-equipped and unable to do anything to halt or repair the damage. I didn't own the coal fired power stations or control the major polluting industries, and neither did I condone the millions of cars that were daily adding to the problem. I couldn't stop the clearing of forests or the raping of the land in countries far from my home, so what was I to do?

What could one person do in the face of governments and multinational corporations responsible for such wilful destruction for financial gain? If the people of the world controlled the decision-making powers of government they could use their vote to act, but I recently learned that governments have become a law unto themselves and little more than puppets of big business. The common man was now powerless, a victim of the greed of a few unscrupulous profiteers. Yet, to my horror, such excuses felt empty. Surely someone could do something to save our earthly home. But what?

CHAPTER 18

The world we live in is different from how it appears. Most people are merely passengers, unaware of their ongoing manipulation and enslavement.

As the food was served, I sought out Mahonri to hear his comments about Toosa's report. I found him sitting at his usual table, locked in conversation.

"Mr Saomes! It has been some time since we've spoken. How are you progressing?" he asked.

"My dear friend, I've been doing very well, and so it seems have you, but I heard Toosa's remarks and I'm troubled. What did you conclude?" I asked.

"Where should one begin to explain the complexities of the nations?" said Mahonri. "Perhaps young Toosa might explain far better than I. He will speak with us soon. Would you like to be present as he addresses us?"

"I would indeed," I replied.

"In the meantime, perhaps we could give you some background to help your understanding. Please be seated and share our refreshments." Mahonri gestured to the seat beside him. I slid in and sat back, waiting for someone to speak. Mahonri began in his usual gentle tones, but there was a strain in his voice I had not heard before. It was as though he was about to tell me something shocking.

"Mr Saomes, the world we live in is quite different from how most people perceive it. There are unseen forces with secret agendas driving and shaping every aspect of human endeavour. Most people are merely passengers on an unknown journey who barely notice the subtle changes as they unfold. They are unaware of the ongoing manipulation the world is being subject to—or the secretive, faceless forms who maintain control."

"There are groups and individuals who act to gain power over their fellow men. We have spoken of the importance of having the right to choose as soon as we are mature enough to do so, but there are those in the world who would take away that fundamental right. They may have noble intentions and believe their ideas are just, but in carrying them out, they have tried to play God. They have sought to exercise unrighteous dominion over a particular segment of society, in essence, to choose for them, which is contrary to the laws and design of He who created us."

"Many have sought to make gain and prosper at the expense of those who are innocent and vulnerable. The rich and powerful have exploited those who are least able to resist; those who have little choice but to allow themselves to be manipulated because of their impoverished situation."

At these comments I shook my head. "I think I understand your implications, Mahonri, but please be specific. Who or what are you referring to?" I asked.

He continued to speak as though I had not interrupted. "When an individual or group tries to exploit others who are helpless to resist, a number of outcomes logically follow. The strong who aspire to apply their strength unrighteously will rule over those who are weaker. Those who become rich will dominate the poor, and those who have power will seek for more at the expense of those who have little or none. A class structure develops and political elements emerge aimed at addressing the associated struggle. Eventually, the growing inequality results in a divided society."

"Most of the war and bloodshed in the world today is a direct result of 'the many' being dictated to by 'the few', Mr Saomes. Conflict arises when one group within society feels unjustly dealt with because they see others receiving an unfair advantage. The fight for equality ensues and may go on indefinitely. But true equality will never be reached when the existing system is only a negotiated one, because neither party will ever be satisfied."

"But surely equality for all is the goal we need to aim for?" I questioned.

"No, Mr Saomes. Freedom to attain one's own sense of equality is the better way. Freedom is the key. Anything short of freedom of choice is an unacceptable proposition. Being forced to accept someone else's concept of equality is not palatable if we don't agree with their measure of what is fair and reasonable. Legislated equality within a framework of corruption is often akin to legalised slavery. The current focus is to force the people to adopt someone else's concept of freedom—not their own."

"Freedom is individual by nature. Often the same concepts and values are not shared by all. There are many civilisations around the world—and what is precious to some is worthless to others. Not everyone wants the same things, Mr Saomes. For example, not everyone approves of drinking alcohol or coffee. In fact, efforts have been made to ban both substances, with worthy arguments to back them up. But because of the profit to sellers and governments, it is unlikely that the sale of either will be banned anytime soon, irrespective of the problems they cause."

"If we are to find peace and harmony between the different groups, we must acknowledge the differences and allow each of them to evolve and stand alone without interference. In time they will prove their worth and flourish, or they will self-destruct. But each individual society must be allowed to work out their own ends without national or international intervention. The ongoing social engineering towards a 'one world' outcome where everyone is forced to be the same must be stopped."

When Mahonri paused to catch his breath, I interjected quickly. "So, where do we stand at present?"

"Our current world is a melting pot of ideologies, or 'idiotologies' as we say in your language! Most governments are only interested in what they might gain for themselves—not for their people. Governments do what they can to stay in power. That is their primary objective. Once in power they seek to rule rather than to serve. Instead of following the agenda that best helps their citizens, they follow a secret agenda towards a 'one world' government. This ideology is currently struggling in many areas—but if successful it holds the potential to destroy the developed world."

"The nations are ruled by ideology rather than principle, Mr Saomes. The leaders of many countries have lost the will to maintain their nation's independence, so they follow the 'one world' dictum and accept internationalism as being inevitable."

"To bring about such ends they carry out constant reforms by enacting new legislation to conform to international edicts, instead of developing their own policies to better serve the people who elected them. They are spineless traitors, Mr Saomes, driven by twisted ideology. Sadly, their actions are nothing short of treason and total stupidity."

Mahonri stared off into space, deep in thought and shaking his head in sheer exasperation. The idea of placing all our eggs in one multicultural basket was clearly of concern to him, just as it is to many observers and commentators around the world.

"So how do we fix the problems?" I asked. "Obviously, those who are plotting to take control have a significant advantage. How do we fight back?"

"We must get back to the concept of 'government of the people, by the people, and for the people, in every nation'. We believe that peaceable mass protests are the most desirable form of defiance. Of course, the spread of Yuwmahn ideals is the best alternative."

"I was personally involved with the late Mr Gandhi, for example. I also had the privilege of meeting with Mr Mandela and Dr King. Their words and methods are being put into action in many areas of the world as we speak. In fact, we as a people have sent emissaries to key places to bring about non-violent and peaceable uprisings for centuries, and we will continue to do so in the future. We feel it our duty to assist those who are unable to help themselves."

"Mr Gandhi was a great leader and a good man to work with—a man I grew to love most dearly as a friend—a true champion of civil rights. His assassination was a tragedy. His service to his people and the world is unparalleled in our modern era. Of course, the methods and ideas are drawn from Yuwmahn philosophy, but the world salutes such men, which is exactly as we would have it."

"Our most recent struggles are with the Triads, the Mafia, and in the Middle East. All the people need is a purposeful way to express their anger. Once they can speak with one voice, their leaders emerge and they organise themselves—and on to victory. The majority, once united, cannot be silenced for long if their will is strong. The rest, as they say, is history, Mr Saomes."

CHAPTER 19

Should individuals be a product of the state that controls them, or should the state act only as a supporting mechanism to the collective will of the people?

As the afternoon unfolded, Toosa joined us and spoke of many things pertaining to global trends and the state of the world. His closing comments stayed with me as we moved off for the evening meal.

"Socialism is spreading like a plague, steadily infiltrating every country, usurping the rights and sovereignty of people and nations. The international socialist agenda is one of constant reform towards a global outcome—one singular world government controlled by an unelected body of faceless men and women who assume the right to govern the whole world."

Returning with small earthen bowls of the most delectable delicacies, we sat to eat in silence savouring every mouthful. My mind was troubled because I couldn't grasp the urgency of Toosa's message, so I sought clarification of several points when the opportunity presented.

"Toosa, what is the main problem you foresee with the socialist takeover?" I asked.

Toosa took a long swallow of his ginger tea and eyed me curiously. "Are you familiar with the concepts of socialism, Mr Saomes?" he began. "Are you aware that a group of would-be dictators seek to assume control of the majority and manipulate them by various instruments of government as they see fit? Can you see that most of mankind is becoming enslaved to a system that offers them little or no say in how they might live?"

His words threw me. I understood the fundamentals of socialism, but I had not fully appreciated the depth of 'control of the many by the few', as he put it. "I know that socialism is fundamentally a dictatorship where the people are told how to live by those who assume the right to direct them. I'm aware that those in the corridors of power propose to set the future for all, while the people are mere pawns who are forced to accept their lot. But I've travelled through communist China and I've seen for myself how the people are provided for by a system which appears to serve them well."

"When you have a benevolent dictator," continued Toosa, "the people may be well looked after for a time—but they are not free. They cannot choose their own way or decide their own outcomes. They remain subject to the small group of elitists who claim to know what's best for them. Far too often such dictators act predominantly in their own interests, and the people are forced to live in relative poverty and misery to support their lavish lifestyle."

"To be truly free, as we are here in Yuwmah, should be a fundamental human right of everyone around the world. Why should any man propose to force others to follow a predetermined way of life that is not of their choosing? To be the master of one's own destiny is essential to ultimate happiness. Under socialism, the state controls where you live, what you eat, where you work, and what you do. Is that the kind of world you'd rather live in, Mr Saomes?" he challenged.

I remained silent as I weighed the substance of his answer. "You're right of course," came my reticent reply. "I guess I never quite understood the lack of freedom. I enjoyed my time in China, and the people seemed content, but I can see that there was more to their condition than I'd realised."

"There have been those who have misread our condition here in Yuwmah," prompted Mahonri. "They saw us as brainwashed into believing in a system of governance that did not serve us well. They thought us to be ignorant slaves and peasants because we worked in the fields and lived simply, not realising our society is exactly as we would have it be by the conscious and unanimous choice of all. No one controls us here. We are free to choose how we spend our time for ourselves."

"The only mandatory aspect of life in Yuwmah is that every family must make a generous contribution to the welfare of all. If they do not pull their weight, they are asked to leave. No one gets a free ride here. We are all supported by each other, so it's a basic requirement to put forth a little effort to ensure that everyone prospers. But that's all that is asked of us."

"Capitalism, on the other hand, sees the emergence of the 'haves' and the 'have-nots'. Many struggle to survive under such a system, but at least the people are somewhat free to choose their own way."

"Although, to get money, most are reduced to little more than slaves." added Toosa. "Under capitalism, the masters rule the workers because they hold the keys to their wealth and future. As a system of control, capitalism is complementary to the socialist model; and in many ways it is even worse. Governments act to support the capitalist system by drafting laws to keep such a system operational. Labour laws and industrial relations agreements forced into existence by unions and regulated by governments continue to control the wheels of capitalist industry."

"In numerous countries, governments hide the true reasons why they legislate specific laws," continued Toosa. "The Fabian socialists for example, who have secretly taken control of many nations, including your land of Australia, will promote laws which move each country and its people ever closer to the principles of

Fabianism. Similarly, communist or fascist governments will prosper their own particular political leaning by way of the laws they enact. Under such conditions, the people lose all sense of power over the system that controls them."

"In a true democracy, the people collectively decide the rules to live by, irrespective of what other countries may be doing. In essence, under a democratic process, the government is an arm of the people, rather than an oppressive and dominating legislative institution run by a central party machine."

"Elected representatives are supposedly chosen to represent the people, but in recent times, because of party allegiances, modern politicians generally vote along party lines rather than representing the will and wishes of their electorate. Sadly, in most countries, party politics has managed to overthrow the democratic process or render it mute."

"Social democracy, or democratic socialism as it is also termed, allows the people to elect those who rule over them, but under such a system the people don't have a direct voice in how they will be governed. Again, they are subject to manipulation by a particular group or party."

"Under a socialist democracy, politicians do not inform those who elect them of the full truth of the laws they promote. Instead, they embark on their secret agendas and make 'unpopular decisions' that are contrary to the will of the majority. Such policies erode the traditional rights and freedoms of their citizens and twist the national psyche towards socialist ends. This is not as it should be and must be stopped at all cost."

"All around the world, governments and politicians are looked upon with contempt. Many voters have little or no respect for the system or those who administer it, because the politicians are driving the people, when most believe it should be the other way around."

"Recently, many governments have won power by the smallest of majorities, while others have been forced to enter coalitions or power-sharing arrangements. This is clear evidence that a huge percentage of the people are not content with the system they find themselves being governed by. In most cases, specific issues matter less than overall philosophies, and far too many votes are cast for the best of a bad bunch."

Mahonri moved to comment. "The first question at the centre of any choice of government or political process is: Should individuals become a product of the state that controls them, or should the state act only as a supporting mechanism to the collective will of the people?"

"In other words, should the people be told how to live by those who propose to know what is best for them, or should the people be given the right to determine their own outcomes?"

"If we follow the Socratic or Aristotelian models of government which underpin our current world, the general populous would be treated as though they have no capacity to govern themselves towards any worthwhile outcomes. Socrates and Aristotle proposed that the people should be forced to surrender to the dictatorship of a small group who presumed to know what is best for all mankind. While this ideal flies in the face of the concept that every person should be free to choose and determine their own destiny, such a system has continued almost unbroken through the ages from the time of the ancient Greeks. Unfortunately, this idea remains the central construct of most societies around the world to this very day."

"We may well ask why such a model has continued through the centuries when it is obviously not advantageous to most of the population. The answer is simple. From the mouths of those in control—if we want to manipulate the masses we must centralise power, so that when we control the king, we also control the kingdom."

"There is however, a second question that is rarely asked, whose answers may have far wider implications for mankind: Should the whole of society be compelled to live under the same set of rules, or could we create different local laws for distinct or differing groups?"

"Do we create a giant melting pot where people holding differing beliefs are forced to co-exist in the same locality under the same laws? Do we force Christians to live next to Muslims or Buddhists or Satanists? Or, do we propose to have each distinct group form their own enclaves and govern themselves according to their specific values? Similarly, do we allow the drug takers to establish their own enclaves and 'do their own thing', and the homosexuals and transgender people to do the same? Is society enriched when we allow each distinct group to separate and establish unique local rules and regulations to govern themselves among their own?"

"The key question we ask in Yuwmah is: How do we create a world where everyone can find the greatest happiness—to live at the very pinnacle of human potential?"

"The Yuwmahn way is to establish differently determined societies, wherein the people choose how they will be governed and form their own societies and structure their local laws accordingly. Such a condition would allow those who value the principles of socialism to live that way if they so desire, while also allowing those who wish to govern themselves democratically to have the right to do so nearby."

"Furthermore, the different aspects of life that exist within our current multicultural communities could become the principal themes of particular enclaves, established specifically for those who wish to practise any form of variation from that of the majority."

"So Caucasians for example, who wish to live in a 'white only' society would be free to do so by passing a local law that denies members of any coloured race from entering or joining their community. Indeed, every other race who wishes to keep themselves together to the exclusion of others could exercise the same right. Those who are happy to live in a multiracial or multicultural system could also exercise such freedom."

"The key to making such a system possible is to grant each enclave the right to make and enforce their own local laws, which includes the right to expel anyone they are uncomfortable with. The first law for every community would then become, 'fit in or leave'. By this method the people could gather in like-minded groups, where peace and social harmony stands the greatest chance of flourishing."

"Such a system would also allow and encourage social diversity, and offer every individual the opportunity to live in the environment that suits their own particular definition of contentment."

CHAPTER 20

Yuwmahn society is based on the Five Pillars of Universal Wisdom: a complete system of governance for self, family, and community.

The evening meal was the usual feast. As we shared the chilli chocolate drink that was their speciality, I felt to press for further understanding of the Yuwmahn way of governance.

"So gentleman, your method of administration here in Yuwmah ... How do you govern yourselves?" I asked to no one in particular.

Toosa was quick to offer his thoughts. "Our city is based on a plan as taught by the Divine One, Mr Soames. His plan of governance sets forth the fundamentals of our way of life. Of all the methods of governance around the world, we know ours is superior because it has stood the test of time."

"As you know, we have no poor or needy here, and neither do we have any sign of slavery. Ours is a classless society. We are all 'free to be'," he added. "No one stands over anyone, and no one gets a free ride or the right to rule over others because they were born as heir to a throne or dictatorship."

I nodded my understanding, but I wanted to get to the detail. "So what is your system of governance called, Toosa," I asked, "How would you describe it?"

"Our system of governance is known as the Mayan Order of Yuwmah, Mr Saomes, because we stem from the original Mayans. We of this city originated from the Olmecs and Toltecs. Both civilisations were considered the most advanced societies on earth at the time of their presumed disappearance. But of course, we never disappeared! We simply dispersed to several new centres because our mother city had become too large and prosperous!"

"The people of the time chose to relocate their homes and their centre of learning. We are their descendants, and the learning goes on among us as it did among them. The name 'Yuwmah' has ancient roots, but we are a modern and progressive city."

"So is there a set of basic tenets of your system of governance?" I asked.

"Our system is based on the Five Pillars of Universal Wisdom, Mr Saomes. Each pillar of wisdom represents a standard or agreement we will not compromise. Each pillar influences all of our most important choices, and serves as the central aspect of who we are as individuals and as a people."

"The Five Pillars are broadly translated as: Faith, Peace, Honesty, Mercy, and Love—concepts of great significance. Each contributes to the bearing up and ennobling of our soul, our civilisation, and our world. Indeed, the Five Pillars of Universal Wisdom form the foundation of all happiness!"

My eyes widened as Toosa continued, "The most fundamental ethos of the Yuwmahn people would be best expressed by the simple phrase—'Advance the Yuwmahn Spirit'. The foundations of Yuwmahnism are centred upon the advancement of individual and collective happiness and are designed to create the best possible environment for happiness to flourish. Such an ethos can be measured by feelings of satisfaction, contentment, and fulfilment."

"In contrast, the capitalist ethos, which has spread around the world like a cancer, is designed to promote consumerism. Its success is measured by company profits and the wealth of those who promote it. Human happiness does not feature as a consideration in a capitalist society. In fact, company profits often swell as a result of human enslavement and exploitation. This is the direct opposite of the Yuwmahn ethos."

"Likewise, the socialist control by governments is a dictatorship—the control of the many by the few. Under both systems, the people are at the mercy of the powerful, who set themselves to determine the collective future of all. By the unconscionable use of the instruments of government, the people are controlled: by a legal system involving police, military, and the imprisonment or death of those who refuse to comply," added Toosa.

"But let us be clear about one crucial point. The prevailing ethos we find ourselves living under should not have the capacity to unduly influence or overpower the human spirit. Each of us should enjoy the right to remain free to choose the path we will walk and the condition of our own soul. A worthy ethos and a supportive system of government controlled by the people will help keep the masses from difficulty and harm. But they must be given the right to choose and act for themselves, to do what is required to be happy on their own terms. We are not here to please the state or to feed and support those who feel they have a right to rule, Mr Saomes."

I exchanged glances with several of those seated around the table. All appeared to be united in their commitment to the Five Pillars. Toosa continued with a fresh burst of enthusiasm.

"As Yuwmahns, our central focus is on the long term happiness and quality of life of our people. We do not live to work or to increase company profits. Neither do we work to live or to just 'get by'. Our society does not give rise to a situation where any individual must carry enormous responsibility for others or cope with any form of significant stress. Instead, our community is set up to allow everyone to experience immense personal freedom and the highest quality of life."

"A Yuwmahn society provides protection from the things we don't need, and regulates our choices so that if we must choose at all, we choose between good and better—not between good and bad. It's easier for us to choose what is right and best, because all choices in Yuwmah are inherently good."

"Out in the world, people are bombarded with temptations. They are often pressed to act in a way they will regret later, which is contrary to their best interests. Such temptations are rife because there is always someone who wants to make money by exploiting human weakness."

"Advertising is such a ubiquitous force in the world. The people are constantly tempted with a few moments of pleasure. They are encouraged to indulge themselves by borrowing money to buy expensive goods and holidays, eating and drinking to excess, and wasting time on pointless entertainment—often with the clear knowledge that they may pay a huge price in the future. But why should they care about tomorrow when they are encouraged to live only for today!"

"There is no such pressure or temptation in Yuwmah, Mr Saomes. Everyone wants to be healthy and happy, which comes to us tomorrow by making wise choices about how we live today. The system here is designed for our optimal benefit, so all we need to do is follow the Yuwmahn way."

"Around the globe, people face temptation at every turn. Their minds are flooded with questionable information: on television and radio, on signposts and billboards, and online. They are forced to deal with the sights, the sounds, and smells of dangerous distraction, assaulting their eyes, ears, and nostrils as they walk down every street or sit in front of their flashing screens."

Mahonri waved his hand in agreement. "Of course choosing wisely becomes easier if we can study the possibilities and decide how we will choose or act before facing particular situations. People are capable of tremendous self-control if they are motivated to put their mind to it, so they can generally learn to govern themselves wisely if they strive to. If the system of governance is good and fair to all, we don't need leaders telling us what to do or how to act. We know how to act for ourselves."

"Self-control is the best form of governance, Mr Saomes. But we have always found that it is much wiser to avoid or remove temptation than to face it often and have to choose the right way over and over again. Yuwmahn society is organised in such a way that it is difficult to be unhappy because our way of life minimises the opportunity for bad choices, openly protecting us from undue sadness and regret."

We sat for a time as I tried to make sense of what was said. I could see that their system of self-governance was all encompassing, and based upon the will and wishes of the collective mind. However, I hadn't grasped the true nature of the Five Pillars or how they formed the heart of all things. My next question caused Mahonri to think deeply before answering, but once begun, he continued unrestrained at a pace I found difficult to follow.

"Yuwmahn society is based on the Five Pillars of Universal Wisdom: a complete system of government for self, family, and community. Each pillar is unique and distinct, but translation to any tongue from the Adamic language is difficult."

"Perhaps we should commence our explanation of the nature of the pillars with the elements of our system that have been introduced in part to other cultures over the centuries. Most people have heard the battle cry of the French Revolution for example. It comprised three central aims: Liberty, Equality, and Fraternity. These ideals became the cornerstones of the American Constitution. You may also be familiar with the four pillars of Buddhism and the Edicts of Ashoka."

"Each of these adaptions of the Five Pillars of Universal Wisdom is a condensed or abbreviated version of the Yuwmahn ethos, but none comes close to the complete Yuwmahn concept."

"The Christian world acknowledges Ten Commandments as the central tenets of their belief system. These ten principles came separately into the world and formed the basis of Jewish law and society for thousands of years. They have no direct link to any

Yuwmahn influence, although they embrace similar concepts because they came from the same source."

"Each pillar is a concept that promotes a law or agreement which is intertwined with the other agreements so that no single pillar exists alone or separate from any other. They are so entwined that violating one will impact on the other four."

"I will try to articulate the Five Pillars as best I can," said Mahonri, "but each one contains concepts that are not part of your culture or language, so it may be difficult to describe them in terms you will readily understand."

"The first pillar we call 'Rata': the bread of life—which connotes equanimity, mental stability, and emotional composure; personal restraint, calm, courtesy, self-control and self-mastery. In a way, it can be translated as liberty or freedom to do whatever we want as long as we control ourselves within the limits of propriety and respectability. Its opposite is self-indulgence, lack of control, disregard for the feelings of others, and selfishness."

"This pillar refers to governing ourselves in a manner that makes us and our actions acceptable and inoffensive to those around us. It is all about bridling our appetites and passions, choosing our words carefully, measuring our conduct and monitoring our demeanour. When we practice the concepts of the first pillar we become truly free while allowing others the same privilege."

"By applying the principles of Rata, we learn to control ourselves so that none will be offended, disadvantaged, disenfranchised, or negatively affected as a result of our actions. In short we cease to be unpleasant, loud, obnoxious, judgemental or discourteous."

"Rata answers the basic question of 'what manner of person ought we to be'. Its single word descriptor is 'faith', because without faith in a supreme power we could justify doing whatever we liked. We could eat, drink and be merry with no self-control and live like the animals because ultimately, it wouldn't matter—for tomorrow we die and that would be the end. But we know death is not the end, so we are compelled to walk in faith, and control ourselves appropriately for the betterment of all."

"The second pillar we call 'Charros': the essence of life—which connotes compassion, the desire to alleviate suffering; benevolence, the desire to help those in need; charity, the act of giving to others and asking nothing in return; and kindness, the act of putting the needs of others before our own."

"When practised openly, this pillar relates in part to the western concept of giving, but in our language we label it as 'peace'. Its opposite is uncaring, lack of concern or consideration, contention, unfairness or cruelty, all of which seed disharmony, even to the point of war."

"This pillar refers to cultivating a generous spirit and becoming a peace-maker, of freely giving or helping those who are disadvantaged, less fortunate, or suffering. It invokes the ideal of standing against the wrongs and injustices of the world and encourages genuine concern for those in need."

"If people across the world practised the concepts of Charros, everyone would have every human need fulfilled, and all would live in peace. Charros also promotes the sentiment of the commandment 'do unto others as you would have them do unto you'."

"The third pillar we call 'Argoll': the breath of life—which connotes pure knowledge, truth, integrity, clarity of thought, and complete disclosure. We have labelled Argoll as 'honesty'. Its opposite is unfair advantage, deception, trickery, dishonesty, lying to others and especially to ourselves. Argoll encompasses the commandments not to steal or bear false witness, not to rob others of their self-respect or dignity, and not to touch or take that which is not ours."

"The fourth pillar we call 'Meres': the treasure of life—which connotes forgiveness, and entails a deep sense of justice. In a way, it also relates to the feeling of community and fraternity, but we label it as 'mercy' because it fulfils the requirement to temper justice with merciful judgement. Its opposites are akin to holding grudges, revenge, and spitefulness."

"The fifth pillar we call 'Barros': the strength of life—which connotes patience, tenderness, gentleness, and meekness. We label Barros as 'love', because each of the attributes related to Barros promote a deep love of self and of our fellow man. Its opposite is forcefulness, harshness, brutality, stress or pressure."

"All of these words have meaning in your language, Mr Saomes, but the direct translation falls short of the true depth of the principles contained therein. I should also emphasise that each pillar can be regarded as a single entity, but in reality each is only a part of a much greater whole, forming a synergistic order that enlarges each component exponentially."

"Can you see from this brief account, Mr Saomes, that our every thought is channelled into five compartments, to be analysed in five different ways, and viewed from five different angles before it is acted upon? Furthermore, it is a foreign concept to Yuwmahnism to treat our own as anything other than a friend. To profit from our dealings with another, especially to their detriment and our advantage, is not conceivable to us," came Mahonri's gentle voice. "We could never be in business to trade for profit among ourselves. Because of our adherence to the principles of the Five Pillars we would end up giving everything away! But we wouldn't mind as long as everyone was content and living in harmony together," he smiled.

"But of course, this brief and singular synopsis is only the beginning of the full concept of the Five Pillars," continued Mahonri.

"There's more?" I queried.

"Oh yes!" came the expansive reply. "Whole volumes have been written about each pillar, but many volumes have been dedicated to their combinations. Only by combining them do we see their greater value and power."

"To fully understand the Five Pillars and their relationship to each other, we arrange them in a pentagon or circle. By way of example, once arranged in the order I related them, we can examine the Promoting Cycle where each pillar promotes or overflows into the next. Then we can examine other combinations such as the Enhancing and Cautioning Cycles. There are many ways to combine the five as you set them in a circular sequence or upon a five-sided cube."

My expression must have been sufficient to show my continued interest, so Mahonri launched into further explanations and examples.

"The courtesy and self-control of Rata within one's heart and mind promotes and overflows into a sense of generosity and giving, and a feeling of equality and fairness towards others as found in Charros, which in turn promotes honesty and pure thoughts as in Argoll, which promotes mercy and forgiveness as in Meres, which promotes Barros, gentleness and patience towards others, which further promotes a greater sense of Rata, the control of self for the benefit of others.

So, when arranged in a circle, we have the Promoting Cycle where each pillar overflows into the next."

"Similarly, we can consider the Enhancement Cycle which is found by referring to each second pillar in a clockwise direction. In this manner, control of self enhances honesty and truth, which enhances gentleness and patience, which enhances greater equality and fairness, which enhances forgiveness and mercy, which further enhances our self-control and self-mastery."

"We can also look at the Cautioning Cycle which highlights our failure in each of these areas. This cycle is the antithesis of the Enhancement Cycle. We find the Cautioning Cycle by considering each second pillar in an anticlockwise direction around the pentagram."

"In this manner, a realisation that we sometimes fail to control ourselves should help us understand that others are not always perfect, requiring greater mercy and forgiveness. So, if we are to be forgiven ourselves, we need to be more forgiving of others. When we fail to forgive others, we may find ourselves being less sensitive to the needs of others as set out in Charros, which in turn may lead us to be harsh with them, which is the opposite of Barros. Harshness often leads to a less than honest assessment, which is the opposite of Argoll, which reflects a lack of self-control as in Rata. Thus the Cautioning Cycle highlights our short-comings and shows man's insensitivity to our fellow man, and our general lack of understanding of others."

A brief pause from Mahonri saw Toosa jumping in eagerly. "My personal favourite is the Balancing Cycle where we examine the effects of too much or not enough of each element. Too much self-control or Rata causes anger and resentment, which is the opposite of Barros, the pillar immediately to the left. But not enough self-control causes a lack of Meres, which is two pillars to the left, and so forth around the circle. Can you see the relationships emerging, Mr Saomes?"

"The overarching maxim of the collective concept of the Five Pillars sets happiness as the final outcome," continued Mahonri. "It comes from a sense of universal harmony, which arises as we learn to balance each of the five universal wisdoms. In other words, we need to find a balance between 'not enough' and 'too much' in each of the five areas. As long as each area remains balanced between those two extremes, we will be happy and live in peace."

"Therefore, at the very centre of the circle of pillars is Harmony and Balance, which we refer to as the 'sixth element'. When we respect each pillar equally, we will find true harmony between the five aspects. This brings us to a greater sense of balance in our decisions and our lives. The ultimate outcome is happiness—which inevitably flows from respecting and balancing each of the five universal concepts."

"So you can see that individually and collectively these pillars provide a framework for the principles that underpin our society and every decision made therein. If each of these pillars were at the centre of every thought, decision, and action—what a different world we would create, what a different life we would live, and what untold happiness we might enjoy."

"Every individual, every family, and every community should give consideration to these principles, and develop their own master plan for human progress. When we have a desire to take control of ourselves and make plans for our future, I can think of no better place to start than to develop our own system of self-government based on these principles."

"The Five Pillars create a simple yet all-encompassing ethos which applies to every situation and circumstance. These are eternal principles; timeless and immutable. Any entity which rests upon them has the capacity to become a source of infinite power, for truly the collective concept empowers all things, both on earth and in the heavens!"

"The Five Pillars of Universal Wisdom form the basis of a set of agreements that govern the entire universe, Mr Saomes. They are respected by the stars and planets and keep them in their course. They manifest themselves in the web of nature, and constitute the very essence of life! If every man learned to see his brother through such eyes, there would be no war—only peace and goodwill."

We sat in silence as the words echoed through our minds. I had little understanding of the depth of their intimations, but those around me bowed their heads in absolute respect for the ideals so passionately articulated. No one spoke as each man paid silent homage, as though each word and thought was sacred and holy.

Together we were reverencing something remarkable: akin to the force that sparked creation, the light at the dawn of life, the source of all matter, and the power that controls all things—an energy emanating from the centre of space and time around which the vastness of the universe revolves—even the substance and power of the very throne of God.

CHAPTER 21

Our world has not unfolded to where it is by accident.
Those in control have a well-defined plan
that is simple and effective.

Several weeks later I found myself chopping wood at the back of the grain store with Jengin, a tall young man with an infectious smile. We discussed many things, and I was amazed that one so young had such a positive outlook.

At the completion of our task Jengin picked up his axe and prepared to leave. As a closing comment he made the following observation.

"It matters not what happens outside the walls of our city, Mr Saomes. Actually, it matters very little what happens outside the walls of our own homes. In our homes we have the opportunity to create our own piece of Heaven, as I have with my sweetheart. No one can spoil that special place except us. My home is my palace, yet we have no servants because we serve each other. The family must be recognised as the fundamental unit of society rather than the individual. Until we re-establish that concept around the world, I perceive that mankind will continue to struggle."

Later that afternoon I sought out Toosa who had become a good friend and asked him to explain what Jengin meant. His answer amazed me.

"The current world is all about focusing on the rights and choices of the individual, Mr Saomes. This is sad because an individual outside the framework of a family is often consumed with personal gratification and all the destructive passions and flaws one might name. At times, everyone needs others to keep them balanced and focused."

"The family is a far more stable and formidable unit than an individual. Only when we put the individual into the context of a family, do we find a more disciplined and self-regulating person. As part of a family the individual has a stronger and more substantial foundation, and greater strength and capacity because they have others to support and guide them."

"We learn most about ourselves as members of a family, especially when we are called upon to serve others. We also learn to be more Godly when we work within the confines of a family structure. Until you are married, you will not fully appreciate how you have to control yourself so that both you and your companion benefit. Self-control is the key. Marriage should be a synergistic arrangement that is considerably enhanced by the addition of children. However, for it to work as it should, we must learn to govern ourselves for the advantage of all."

Another week passed quickly. I had developed an unquenchable thirst for knowledge, spending every available minute in the library reading as much as I could. I learned anew of past and present events and the impact they had on the people of the world. I also learned about the complexities of nations: of greed, power and subversion, traditions and customs, and the conflicting values of various cultures. As I opened my mind to the different perspectives, my outlook broadened.

As an example of my new learning, I include a brief excerpt from my awkward translation of an old leather-bound Yuwmahn history book known as '*The Interpretations of Ragor*', which was written several hundred years ago. It reads as follows:

Many philosophers have mused that a world composed of such a variety of nationalities and societies, each evolving in general isolation, was always destined to be a mishmash of ideas and ideologies. The only common thread is the emergence of a system whereby the rich rule over the poor and the strong dominate the weak.

In truth, our current international discord is not the result of a lack of organisation or direction as we might think. In fact, our world is precisely as it was designed to be. Every step of change over many centuries has been secretly engineered and orchestrated by the faceless men who propose to take control of the entire world.

Those in control have a well-defined plan that is simple and effective. They aim to sow discord among the nations, and especially among the people. They intend to take from every individual their inalienable right to choose—to seize the opportunity to decide for them, and thereby control them.

To aid their efforts, they strive to rob the ordinary man of his ability to think and act for himself to such a degree that he becomes susceptible to manipulation—at which point he loses control of his own destiny and unknowingly surrenders to those who would enslave him. This is supposedly done for his own good because it is widely believed among the 'elite masters' that the common man lacks the capacity to govern himself for his individual or collective betterment.

So, a small and unelected body of powerful men have set out to take control of the world and everyone in it, to direct our future course and govern the population as they see fit. The most remarkable part of this takeover is that most people are unaware of their progressive enslavement. This sinister exercise, conceived centuries ago, has been carried forward in such a gradual way that generation after generation fail to realise they are further surrendering themselves to the forces set to bear upon them.

—The Interpretations of Ragor

The more I read about the exploitation of the many by the few, the more I was determined to fight back. I became enraged at the corruption of religious and government favours, bought with bribes to produce predetermined outcomes by those who stood to gain from the injustice.

I also learned that the greatest crimes were not only overlooked by law enforcement agencies and crime authorities but were often perpetrated by them. I found significant evidence to indicate that public servants had become the public masters, many of them infiltrating key positions of authority to bring about predetermined and malicious ends.

From another curious book called *'The Prophesies of Ilam'*, whose cover was pure gold, with leaves made of brass, I read the following poem:

> *The time is fast approaching*
> *when a maleficent mist shall move upon the land;*
> *descending like a cloak of corruption*
> *and a cloud of catastrophe*
> *spreading like a malignant cancer,*
> *consuming all who might stand against it;*
> *engulfing ideas and ideals,*
> *enslaving families, communities,*
> *cities and nations,*
> *hiding faceless men and secret forces*
> *who move invisibly within its silent veil.*

JOURNEY TO YUWMAH

It will be as a mist of darkness and deception,
of mysticism and deceit.
Within its shadows will emerge plans afoot
and schemes in motion,
silently gathering momentum,
sending forth their treacherous tentacles,
promoting wicked ways
and prospering their private purposes.

Within the mist, truth will be twisted and overshadowed.
Falsehood shall come forth
to be openly promoted and paraded
as a viable and acceptable alternative.
All the world will have the right to choose and embrace it,
and none will dare to condemn for fear of retribution.
The people shall be free to accept, but not to reject—
subtly brainwashed and conned into believing
they must accommodate every whim
of foolishness and immorality,
without discrimination
between right and wrong
or good and evil.

And nations shall lose their way,
and terrorism shake the entire earth.
The people will live in fear,
and secretly despise those who offend them,
but shall not openly accuse.
And wars will be fought in the hearts of men,
with untold casualties,
and the suffering shall be greater than a mortal soul can bear;
and human happiness shall be mocked and utterly destroyed.

Only honest truth can lay bare such corruption,
and thwart the schemes of malicious men.
Light must be shone into darkness.
Every plan, plot, and ploy, must be illuminated.
Every vine of villainy must be rooted out,
and every attempt at social domination must be crushed.
Every effort to subvert that which is good
and right and virtuous must be exposed.
Fundamental rights and freedoms must be maintained.
The right of all men to choose their own destiny
must be held inviolate.

The footnote read as follows:

The subtle control and enslavement of the many by the few must end. This is our eternal task: our duty and mission throughout mortality. Let every man who learns the truth teach his neighbour, and let every voice speak openly of the fate awaiting mankind if they fail to defend and preserve their God-given rights and freedoms.

—The Prophesies of Ilam

On a more personal note, I read several books, which pricked my conscience to the core. Recently I'd come to know myself as arrogant, and at times brash, insensitive, impatient, and excessively demanding. As I pondered the following, I was humbled by the weight of my own realisation that I was not the kind of man I now desired to become.

A brief excerpt from *'The Book of Eli'*:

'What Manner of Man'

We bless the world and make it better by actions taken collectively and individually. If man aspires to lasting happiness, he must put off every human fault and failing, and become as a new and better man: brave, courageous, resilient, patient, kind, selfless, compassionate, gentle, humble, generous, industrious, forgiving, and honest to himself and others.

He must develop the strength to resist temptations, keeping himself from being proud, arrogant, resentful, discourteous, or lazy.

When provoked he must possess the power to rise up against injustice, to confront his accusers, to defend the innocent, to rebuke those who bear false witness, and expose those who would practise deception.

He must develop a powerful and enquiring mind, a strong back and shoulders, a firm yet gentle hand, a soft and pious heart, and an eye single to truth and right.

He must become the master of his own soul, controlling his urges, curbing his temper, and bridling his passions and his wants.

For his own benefit and for all who look to him for support, he must be true to his word, committed to his cause, and focussed upon his goal.

He must be pure of mind and body, that regret may not cripple him, that selfishness may not overtake him, that envy may not devour him, that ambition may not blind him.

He must stand for justice, press for mercy, fight for victory, sue for peace, and seek for wisdom.

Above all, he must be filled with a love for truth, that he may be ever true to himself and to others, that he may develop such love and compassion for even the least deserving of those he serves.

—The Book of Eli

As the refiner's fire burned within me, I felt the anger disperse. My previously obnoxious nature began to shrivel, leaving me as a new and purified character of greater depth, compassion, and inner strength, than I'd ever known.

From the following letter penned by a loving father to his son, I gained a deeper understanding and appreciation for all that I was and everything I had become—grateful and thankful for the blessings my life had afforded me.

From *'The Wisdom of Uhdu the Fisherman'*
(as written to his son Amon):

A significant contribution everyone can make to improve the world is to improve themselves—to be better and do better day by day.

Therefore, be as the great river: deep and silent, flowing meekly along with quiet purpose and determination to the sea, to take your rightful place amid the great waters of the world—which is your destiny.

Be not as the small stream: gurgling harshly, complaining loudly over every undulation, lying stagnant and bitter in pointless pools to be evaporated and lost—serving no worthwhile purpose or benefit to yourself or others.

Be as the river reeds: standing tall above tranquil waters, bending as the torrents of life rush by—but never sinking or breaking—immovable against the pressures upon you, buoyed by a clear conscience and a pure heart, unsullied by guilt or shame, to stand resolute, strong-rooted and hardy against the changing seasons of life.

Be not as driftwood: carried along by wind and current, moving without purpose or direction, tossed and buffeted through the shallows, rushing through narrow ways, constantly at the mercy of the elements.

When I was a young man I tried to be as the great eagle: flying high to see every possibility, to swoop with speed to seize the prize with mighty talons and carry it off to victory.

As an older man I try to be like the graceful gull: to glide patiently on currents of gentle breeze and quietly choose my treasures, to descend to their side, to study them closely with tilted head, and consider my options carefully before making my final choice.

I am but a humble fisherman. I seek not for glory or aggrandisement, only to live simply and enjoy my charmed existence, to provide well for my family, and fulfil my duties to the best of my ability. The stars of the night are my jewels; the moonlight upon the waters is my paradise. My boat rocks gently to cradle me and I sleep in peaceful dreams.

I seek not to exercise power to control or direct others, or to force my will upon them. I respect the right of every man and woman to determine their own course through life. I respect the earth and the sky, the changing of the seasons and the passing of years. I cherish the waters that give me sustenance. I take no more than I need. I sleep well because my conscience is clear and my heart is pure. I find joy beyond measure in the simple aspects of daily living, and appreciate my place in this wonderful world as part of the great cycle of nature and the unfolding of the universe.

—*The Wisdom of Uhdu the Fisherman*

My new-found knowledge changed me. Over the course of the coming weeks and months, the hard exterior and false facades so commonly portrayed in the west began to melt away. All the protective mechanisms, the distrust and selfish inclinations that many adopt to survive were no more. I became open and self-assured, refreshed and invigorated, cleansed and unburdened. Each day I became more patient and caring, more inclined to wait and consider the needs of others ahead of my own. Moreover, I soaked up every new ideal with a thirst I could not quench.

One particular evening I lay on my bunk, reflecting upon the proposition that back in my world I was regarded as a successful journalist, widely respected as an authority on many subjects. Academics and politicians had heralded my articles as works of substance. I accompanied statesmen and diplomats, interviewed kings and presidents, and moved around the globe as though it was a very small sphere. Yet, how innocent I had been, and how uninformed! How narrow was my vision, how childlike my approach, and how pointless my efforts; for ultimately, what good had come of it?

I also considered my decision to flee from Yuwmah before it became so desirable that I might walk away and hide from the outside world forever. Upon my return that same evening I was carried over an invisible line, transported beyond that place and time to a new beginning. I became part of something fresh and vibrant that was also ancient and timeless—something ethereal that embodied the very essence of the soul of man.

I now felt as though this place and I had fused together; I had become part of it and it was part of me. The whole Yuwmahn experience was a living example of the 'brotherhood of man'—the melding together of like-minded individuals who had come to accept a shared ethos and apply themselves to the improvement and edification of one and all.

Whatever the reason, life in Yuwmah was wonderfully freeing. I had grown to love and appreciate the beauty, the elegance, and the simplicity. My body was strong and healthy, my mind open and filled with meaningful thoughts, my heart pure and sensitive. In truth, Yuwmah and all it stood for had not only permeated my being, but at times I felt my soul transformed like an opening flower. My mind had become older and wiser beyond my years. Would I ever go back to the life I once knew? I could at any time—but why would I ever want to? Why indeed!

CHAPTER 22

We are spiritual beings—intelligent and eternal ...
One of the greatest downfalls of man is the lack
of understanding of his spiritual self.

Springtime in the mountains was glorious. I enjoyed an afternoon picnic with Mahonri and his extensive family. We sat on bamboo rafts secured along the river's edge. The day was unusually hot forcing even the most hardy to retreat to a cool spot. Many swam and played in the emerald green water. Mahonri seemed less sprightly than usual, his comments brief and contributions few. Eventually he excused himself to return to his abode to rest more comfortably. To my surprise, my offer to accompany him was met with welcome, indicating the seriousness of his condition, or so I thought.

Arriving at his door he invited me inside, an honour I was not prepared for. Misha had acknowledged our departure with a brief wave. As we entered, Mahonri made for his favourite chair and lay back to rest his head against the intolerable humidity.

"Let me assure you, Mr Saomes, my health is fine. I simply felt a desire for solitude. I'm not at my best in such heat. Your concern for my welfare is comforting, and I am pleased we now have time to ourselves away from the chatter."

Misha arrived soon after with a pot of kombucha tea.

"Ahhh ... this will rejuvenate the body, mind, and spirit. A marvellous elixir indeed. Just what we need on such a day!" Mahonri smiled. I noted the frailty of his frame and the labour of his breathing; his advanced years showed plainly in his eyes. My silent stare must have alerted him to my questioning mind.

"Mr Saomes," he asked gently, "what troubles you?"

My eyes surveyed his wizened face. At first I was reluctant to speak, feeling to spare him the burden of answering. My hand twitched to wave the moment away, but his withered hand reached for mine and clasped my fingers.

"What troubles you my friend?" he asked again firmly.

I swallowed. "Your comments a moment ago—'the mind of man'," I began, "and 'the things of the spirit'. I don't understand such concepts."

His head rolled back on narrowed shoulders, eyes closing as he inhaled deeply and expressed air through pouted lips. A broad smile made his face shine as if he were pleasantly relieved.

"I can well understand your difficulty with such concepts, my young friend, for little is known of such in the greater world. Quite simply, our spirit gives life to our physical body, Mr Saomes," came the breathless voice. "Our spirit is alive within each of us, filling us with the energy that invigorates all living things. It is an invisible presence, as tangible as our physical self, housing our sense of consciousness and intelligence. Our spirit dwells within our body giving life from the time of our birth to the moment of our death."

"Physicists speak of 'dark matter' because they know there is more to the universe than the sum of all the atoms and heavenly bodies. They have no concept of the nature of such substance because they can't see it—but it is all around us. Spirit is everywhere. It has both mass and intelligence. If acted upon it will react in specific ways. So, when our heavenly parents created spiritual beings, they organised intelligence rather than atoms and molecules as with our physical bodies."

"The human brain is a complex and marvellous organ, but man attributes far too much to it. In fact, the brain remains somewhat of a mystery, only because man tries to make it the centre of all aspects of the spirit: of consciousness, memory, personality, and thinking. Science has no evidence to support such claims, but scientists have nowhere else to lay them, so

237

they attribute everything about us to the mushy mass inside our heads. In basic terms, the brain is a simple organ capable of little more than responding to stimuli from other organs and sensors around the body."

"Our spirit resides within our physical body and gives life to every cell of our entire being. We identify it as our conscious self. Our mind is an aspect of our spirit. The mind interfaces with our brain, but it is part of our spiritual self, not of our physical body. When we injure a part of our brain, we destroy that region of the interface and lose the associated capabilities, but our mind remains whole. At death, our spirit will leave our body, complete with our lifelong learning and memories. Our spirit retains our personality and the ability to remember and reason. Essentially, we are spiritual beings—intelligent and eternal—residing in tabernacles of clay until death frees us from our confinement."

"The gifts of the spirit are many, Mr Saomes. They are more far-reaching and powerful than all of our five physical senses. We have immeasurable powers of perception, intuition and communication, enhanced strength, vision and hearing, and incredible powers of telepathy; even levitation is possible should we care to develop it. One of the greatest downfalls of man is the lack of understanding of his spiritual self and the under-development of his spiritual senses."

"As children, we learn to see with our physical eyes, but few have learned to see with their spiritual eyes. Our spiritual abilities allow us to discern and comprehend truth and detect falsehood. Man, to his detriment, is only focussed on the physical, so he operates with limited capacity. When we learn to develop our spiritual abilities, we can know that which we cannot see, we can feel that which we cannot otherwise know, and we can discern that which only the spiritually enlightened can understand."

"If you cannot perceive what is behind you as plainly as you can see in front, that particular spiritual gift remains undeveloped. If you cannot communicate with the animals, listen to the chatter of the trees or the whisper of the grasses; if you cannot feel the presence and aura of those around you; if you cannot commune with the spirits of your ancestral dead or your unborn children—then clearly you have not learned to harness the powers of the spirit—to comprehend the secrets of nature, or appreciate the true design and majesty of the heavens above."

As was my habit, I lay on my bunk that night and considered Mahonri's comments. I knew of tribes around the world who practised strange forms of magic and performed superhuman feats like walking on a bed of hot coals without burning their feet. I also considered that ghosts and spirits have been part of recorded history since ancient times, with many claiming to see and even communicate with them. I remembered the Maori legend which suggests that our spirit leaves our body when we die, but does not return to Heaven until the body is buried.

I was also well accustomed to the feelings associated with some kind of sixth sense that made me conscious of others around me, and especially of things happening behind me. I felt aware somewhere deep inside, but did not see with my physical eyes. Men through the ages have claimed the ability to walk on water, to levitate themselves off the ground, even to fly onto the roofs of high buildings. Many have performed feats of incredible strength which could not be reasonably explained, such as the woman who lifted a car to save her child from being crushed.

The full moon that night shone down upon me through the sky-window, illuminating my room brightly as I struggled to find sleep. Refusing to block out the heavens I sat up and lay back against the wall. Raising my hands towards my face, I splayed my fingers wide and looked hard at the palms, wondering what powers might be at my disposal if only I knew how to summon them. I pressed my ear against the ancient wall and listened for any word or whisper from the past or from deep inside the earth.

"Do trees have an opinion of the world?" I wondered. "What do trees talk about?" I asked myself aloud. My mind flashed back to my childhood, to a time when I believed that wind was made by the movement of the trees. I had seen it with my own eyes: a forest of towering eucalypts began to sway back and forth together, bending and twisting as their trunks stretched and contorted, the faint whistle of wind rising around me as leaves fluttered to the ground. As the powerful movements of the branches increased, the wind began to howl. Soon, the whole forest became a thunderous thrashing of foliage as I struggled to stand against the awesome power conjured by the movement of the trees—or so I imagined.

That memory brought to mind the truism that what we see and what we believe are not always as they really are. The gifts of the spirit seemed plausible, but they could not be detected or measured by scientific methods. But, the fact that they could not be proven did not diminish their possible existence, or the Yuwmahn faith in their application.

The following morning found me on the lower level of the library. A fascination with my hitherto untapped spiritual capacities had been awakened. I had selected a number of books on the subject from the vast shelves and was clumsily carrying them back to my cubicle.

As I made my way, a troublesome volume sprang from the top of the pile and plummeted to the floor with a heavy thud. Heads turned from every direction. I looked down at the offending volume to avoid the peering eyes. With no free hand to reach out and grab it, I hesitated for the longest moment, wishing it might leap back up and redeem itself, and save me from feeling so foolish.

But alas, to my deepening consternation, the enormous leather-bound volume lay defiantly where it fell. I stood there, frozen to the spot, awkward and helpless, wondering what to do next.

A group of people were congregated nearby at a long table. From the corner of my eye I saw one of them push back their chair, bend to retrieve the book in a smooth motion, and casually step to my side.

"Hello Mr Saomes," came her gentle greeting as she popped the book on top of the stack.

I looked blankly at the womanly apparition before me as she stood in a broad shaft of brilliant light beaming through the window above. She was slim with soft eyes and a narrow nose. Her salt and pepper hair fell neatly around her pleasant face. I determined she was perhaps a few years younger than myself, and strangely familiar.

"Have we met?" I blurted.

"We met briefly, but we were never formally introduced. You were with Master Mahonri. I tended to you as you regained your strength, on the upper level, near the observatory."

"I am Panqara," she added shyly after a brief pause. "I am pleased you have recovered."

"Thank you," I heard myself reply. "I have little recollection of our meeting, but I thank you for your kindness."

Through the awkward moment that followed, I found myself transfixed by her presence. There was a certain nobility about her, a composed elegance and grace—and there was an energy—an invisible force that held me captive until she smiled her farewell.

I manoeuvred my pile of books without further incident and deposited them on the sturdy wooden desk. Turning to sit, I looked back across the crowded room. My eyes searched the rows of faces but my apparition was nowhere to be seen. I opened the first book and browsed the contents, my gaze distracted by distant forms as they came and went. Throughout the morning, and for several mornings thereafter, I kept a silent vigil, but the beautiful Panqara had vanished.

CHAPTER 23

I have learned first-hand through the course of my long life that you cannot love someone too much.

O ne sunny afternoon, I found myself in the company of Mahonri and his friends at mealtime beneath the canopy of green.

"Mr Saomes, how are you?" came Mahonri's welcoming greeting.

"I am well, Mahonri, and pleased with my progress. I have learned much over these past months and made some close friends along the way. My life has become more rewarding and enjoyable than I ever thought it could be," I replied with enthusiasm.

"And what have you learned, my young friend?" he asked.

"I've learned so much I scarcely know where to begin."

"I am pleased to hear it. And how has this new learning affected you?" he enquired.

"It has changed me forever. I am a new man, transformed beyond description. I feel almost immortal!"

At my flippant remark Mahonri's face clouded. His probing eyes fixed on mine in a way I'd come to know well. He paused and pursed his lips. From experience I knew he was about to say something profound, but this time I thought I might be ready.

"And what will you do with this new learning, Mr Saomes?" came his challenge as he studied me intently, searching my expression for a hint of what I might be thinking. Clearly, I had no answer.

Fidgeting nervously I asked a question of my own. "Mahonri, what does one do with learning?"

"First you must use it to organise your life for your own betterment and security, and then put it to use in ways that benefit others. Knowledge must be applied to something or it is without value. Put it to work, Mr Saomes, to improve lives," came his gentle reply.

"The human mind is more powerful than a nuclear reactor coupled to a supercomputer larger than the moon, yet it is small enough to be housed inside our head. Our eyes, ears, and nose, are like portals. Our senses detect and determine. Words express the thoughts of the mind—and like our mind, our words can be incredibly powerful, having the power to create or destroy. The heart determines what we say and what we hold back. But knowledge, Mr Saomes, is the raw material that empowers the soul. Without knowledge we are powerless to act."

"When our mind is filled with knowledge, we become a powerful and conquering force capable of dominating and devouring those who are less informed. So knowledge is the source of tremendous power, my young friend, which you must now control and put to good use, before it becomes a destructive force within you!"

I stammered, "But surely I have learned nothing new—certainly nothing you are not aware of."

"That is not the point," Mahonri replied firmly. "If you are to become wise and find true happiness, you must apply your knowledge to promote positive outcomes. And let us remember that it is God Himself who is the possessor of all knowledge and wisdom. As we apply the things we have learned and become a greater force for good, we also become more Godlike, which is fulfilling one of the most important measures of our creation."

"Perhaps I should also point out that as we grow in understanding, we must also grow in other ways or we become unbalanced. For example, charity is a necessary ingredient in any pursuit of excellence. It is needed to temper our learning so that all may be edified by the knowledge we gain. Knowledge without a charitable countenance may cause our heads to swell, and we may become excessively proud, even to use our knowledge unwisely or conduct ourselves foolishly. The world is full of educated fools, Mr Saomes."

"Those who lack charity may persecute others for their ignorance or take unfair advantage of them. In such situations knowledge may be used for evil. Any acquisition of knowledge must be tempered with humility and charity. In this way, knowledge can make us wise."

"To grow in wisdom is to conquer one's weaknesses such as pride, envy, and selfishness, and rise above personal ambition in favour of the betterment of all. Self-discipline and self-mastery are the true keys to personal progress, Mr Saomes. Without these attributes we are of little worth or substance, and we risk becoming enslaved by our own foolishness."

"Self-control is also essential as we grow in learning and stature because it invokes a depth of character, which is the true measure of man. Without self-control we become slaves to unholy habits. If we govern ourselves wisely, we are fit to govern families and influence the world positively—but if we are not sober and in control of ourselves, we are not fit to govern swine."

After a pause punctuated by the sounds of eating, I continued more calmly. "Mahonri, where does one apply such learning in a perfect place like Yuwmah? Or does my understanding simply allow me to fit in more comfortably? I know nothing more than everyone else here. In fact, even now I feel like a kindergarten kid among those who've graduated university with the highest honours."

"We use our abilities, talents, and knowledge in our homes and in our community—and further afield as we have the opportunity—but foremost in our homes to benefit our loved ones."

"I see! But I have no wife or family, and I have no immediate plans of having one." At this point, I thought we might break into one of those jovial exchanges about the comical side of being married, but Mahonri was not in a frivolous mood.

At Mahonri's suggestion, we rose from the table and walked for some distance. I expected him to continue our conversation, but he remained aloof. Eventually the silence overcame me and I asked a question that was now at the forefront of my mind.

"Tell me of marriage and family Mahonri. What am I missing by being single and on my own?"

"Ah, Mr Saomes! This is indeed a weighty question which I perceive you have wrestled with for some time!" he exclaimed light-heartedly.

"I have!" I replied. "In my previous life outside the walls of Yuwmah, I had no thought of marriage or relationships. But here, I am constantly confronted by my singleness!"

"So you would hear the full truth, even if it is not pleasant?" he queried.

"Yes—of course!" I replied.

The aged man contemplated his answer before he began to speak.

"When we marry another person, two souls are joined to become 'as one'. Marriage is perhaps the most significant challenge we will ever face, Mr Saomes. By its very nature it can lift us so high we can hardly breathe, or sink us so low that we descend below all things. Being married can be complicated and painful, and yet it can be so simple and incredibly beautiful."

"Every marriage is unique and dependent on the couple involved, so it is sometimes difficult to analyse in broader terms, but in essence, all relationships share a common thread, no matter where you go in the world."

"You see, man and woman are not complete of themselves. None of us has all the attributes needed to be perfect on our own. It is true that we can feel complete on many levels, but we cannot function at our absolute best when we are alone. A far better measure of justice and mercy can be found when two minds work together as one."

"Typically, a man's perspective is different from a woman's. This is one of the main reasons we need each other, to find greater understanding and a finer sense of balance."

"When we draw close to someone, we begin to take their attributes upon ourselves: to think like them, to feel like them, and even to speak and act like them. We may appear to change into someone new, but really they are only bringing out a particular facet of ourselves that was always there."

"Different people bring out different aspects in each of us. My Misha inspires me to be a better man, and for that I am eternally grateful. I like the person I've become because of her. Most of all, we have learned to complement each other so very well."

"We are equal in many ways, but we are not the same. I draw so much from her because she possesses attributes I am not blessed with. Each of us has a measure of every passion, but the amounts vary. We were created to be different, Mr Saomes, so that each might be equipped for their own environment, to suit the tasks they were naturally designed to perform."

"Men are physically stronger and tougher, which allows them to do what men do best. Rough-and-tumble is the natural way of boys from an early age. Women tend to be more soft and tender, and their feelings likewise, which allows them to be at their best in a different environment. Men and women are fundamentally different, Mr Saomes, but when you put the two together, you have a formidable combination capable of far more than each on their own. Together they can achieve greater things and become more accomplished than either one by themselves."

"It is also true that men can nurture children and women can chop wood, but mothering is not natural to most men, and women are typically better mothers because they have an instinctive edge. Men make better fathers who can chop wood faster and with greater ease. Both genders have natural inclinations, so where differences exist it makes sense to allow each to do what they do best. Don't you think?"

Before I could answer, Mahonri continued. "The natural attraction between the sexes is the basis of any relationship. When two people spend time together, a feeling of closeness develops. If we did not have the word 'love', we would probably use the word 'caring'. When two people care for each other, they do and say things that show forth their 'love'. The more we care, the deeper the love. When one ceases to care, the love has died, which is sad indeed."

"But these things you know, Mr Saomes. Surely you have been in love at some stage of your life?" he asked.

"Oh yes!" came my reply. "But my experiences were fleeting, and they didn't end well."

"Like so many before you and so many since!" he replied. We walked on in silence for a time. Mahonri appeared deep in thought, and when he began again, I knew by his tone I was about to hear something special.

"I know the majority of relationships fail these days, but this is not as it should be. I do not wish to attribute blame to either party, but if they knew what they were missing, perhaps they'd try harder to find the better way. The heart of the matter is that each has to want to—day after day and forevermore.

"The key is found in expressing the love we feel in worthwhile ways to keep it meaningful. If both feel loved, they will stay 'in love'. But if one doesn't feel the love, interest will wane because everyone has a fundamental need to give and to receive. If we don't experience both feelings, we will not feel fulfilled."

"Acts of love also promote respect and appreciation. When one loses respect for the other, both are in trouble, and their end is nigh. Indeed, love is like shaving, Mr Saomes! You must attend to it every day or things can become prickly!" said Mahonri, rubbing his wrinkled cheek." In the same manner, a relationship must be kept alive or it will fade and wither like a broken branch."

"Many claim to be 'in love', but few seem to know how to express their love in ways that make it precious. A special feeling comes over us when we feel loved in a real and personal way. But, truly I tell you, bestowing such feelings on others is even more rewarding to the soul than receiving them."

"The hardest part of being married is that nothing stays the same for long," Mahonri continued. "We are always growing and changing: developing new ideas, pursuing new dreams, meeting interesting people, and entertaining new distractions. It is so very easy to go off on a tangent and lose your way. Many allow themselves to wander too far alone in a new direction, and before they realise, they have lost everything that ever mattered."

"There are three great secrets to marriage, Mr Saomes, and I feel to share them with you so you will understand. The greatest secret to building a strong and enduring marriage is to find 'the third way'. When a man and a woman approach anything together, they may see things in different ways. So, if they are wise, they will set aside their own ways and develop 'their' way—a third way agreeable to both. This is the first great secret of any successful relationship. The two must learn to work together to find outcomes that both can own and enjoy."

"The second great secret, Mr Saomes, is to keep yourself lovable. The solution to this challenge may take many forms. Irrespective of what you value in each other, it is essential to be found pleasing and enjoyable, to be a worthy companion, not one who is difficult to be with. Change is ongoing throughout our entire life, so our natural goal is to draw closer together as we age, rather than becoming increasingly unpleasant and drifting apart."

"The third great secret is to dedicate yourself to your spouse and always put them at the centre of your world, and keep them there always! If we allow ourselves to be distracted, whether by ambitions, other people, or daydreams; we move our focus away from the most significant person in our world, away from the one who is the other part of ourselves. In this manner we become divided and lose that special bond."

"You see, Mr Saomes, two people need to work at their relationship and do all they can to keep these three fundamentals in place. The first secret of finding the third way, is difficult to learn, but once achieved it will serve you both well for a lifetime. The second secret, keeping yourself loveable, is both difficult and ongoing. But the hardest of all is the third, which requires a daily re-commitment to a person and an ideal, both of which are constantly changing and unfolding with time. For some, this ongoing challenge becomes overwhelming or nigh on impossible."

Mahonri then stopped and turned towards me. Drawing a deep breath, he placed his hand on my shoulder. "But love, Mr Saomes," he continued, fixing my eyes with his gaze, "is a many splendid thing of unparalleled beauty and joy. When two people have learned to truly love each other, they can work through almost anything. Every marriage has the potential to become a perfect partnership: the most complete surrender, and at the same time the most decisive and valuable victory!"

"Fundamentally, marriage is two people becoming 'as one'. Right now my Misha is at home and I am here—but I feel her presence no matter where I am, as though she is part of me. My first thought is always of her. I have found in her a sense of reason—of purpose and direction that defies description. I am as I am because of her. I feel as I feel because of the way she feels. I think thoughts that are not mine, but ours. She has fused into me and we are no longer two individuals or even two halves. Together we have become one, and I am a thousand times the man I was because of her. If I should lose her, I would not want to breathe, and I may quickly cease to do so."

As Mahonri spoke, I could feel him choking with emotion. All at once, tears fill his eyes and he gripped my shoulder as if he were stumbling.

"When you have known true love, Mr Saomes," he whispered with a trembling voice, "you have experienced the most precious of all things—the absolute pinnacle of happiness."

Without conscious thought I found myself reaching out to embrace him. Mahonri allowed me to draw him in, and for a moment he rested his old head against my shoulder to regain his composure. Drawing apart again, he wiped his eyes with the backs of his hands. I stood motionless, in awe of the depth of love and devotion displayed. Clearly, Mahonri's love for his sweetheart was all-consuming.

"I am sorry, Mr Saomes," he almost laughed. "I have allowed myself to be overcome, for such are my feelings for my Misha and for who I am because of her. Truly I would be a lesser man without her. She is the very heart of me and the foundation of all that I am."

"I have learned first-hand through the course of my long life that you cannot love someone too much! I try every day to show those I care about that they are of value to me. Scripture tells us to show love by both word and deed. So we tell people we love them, but we should also show it. The best part is that love freely given tends to come back manyfold! Such is the substance of it."

"There are some who are so self-centred; they only take, with no thought of giving back. But they are few, and they will learn eventually, we hope! But for the most part, love freely given is like a seed that grows and bears fruit, blessing the lives of many. The essential aspect is to express love and act upon it—not keep it to yourself!"

"Can you imagine what the world would be like, Mr Saomes, if everyone gave freely and lovingly to each other? If we, as couples, as families, as part of a community, could reach a stage where we truly loved one another and gave freely without wanting anything in return—how free each of us would feel—and how fulfilled and blessed might we be! This is the real message of the scriptures and of all we believe which is good—the prime objective the whole world needs to embrace. Mr Saomes! It is such a beautiful plan! Can you not see it? Is it not a marvellous concept!"

I found my mind spinning, but words wouldn't come. Mahonri grabbed my shoulders, and we danced around together as he jostled and shook me. There was so much love within him at that moment that it could scarcely be contained. His smile was radiant as he glowed with joy—and I was privileged to bask in that glow. And from that expression of love, I was warmed somewhere deep inside. My heart swelled to bursting and love became me and filled me, and I was born anew.

CHAPTER 24

*Everywhere you look, the world is at war with itself
and in a worse mess today than ever before!*

On my bunk that night I tossed and turned in restless sleep. Emotions played in my head as I weighed my experiences over the past months. My soul had been enlightened and my vision enlarged. I had so much to give and an overwhelming desire to do so. Without a doubt, I was a better person and far more capable of making a difference than I'd ever been. But how to give back even a portion of what I'd received was more than I could fathom. In Yuwmah, and without a family of my own, the possibilities seemed few to none.

"What does one do in my situation?" I pondered to myself. My potential felt locked up and lifeless, I held so much promise, yet it was silent and without form. I had no voice for expression and no opportunity to set a single idea in motion.

My inclination at that moment was to remain in Yuwmah, but if I did—what good could I do? If I returned to my homeland, how would I fit in? There were many aspects of my former life that no longer mattered, and those that did had changed so much that my entire life would require a complete rethink.

Morning came through the half open sky-window, earlier than I anticipated. I'd slept with my latest conundrum, and on waking I felt dishevelled and quite confused. I lay on my bunk longer than usual, eventually rallied by a smiling Mahonri who called by as he was passing, supposedly on an errand for Misha. There was no gravity in his tone as he asked how I slept.

"Our conversation of yesterday overtook me in the night," I replied, realising for the first time that I'd begun to speak like these people! "I feel as though I'm bursting with potential, but I struggle with the question of what contribution I can make. I have no clear idea of what I might do or where I might do it."

"Mr Saomes!" exclaimed Mahonri. "The world is in a worse mess today than ever before! The peoples of the world have been programmed to believe much that is false and harmful. They are enslaved by a system which robs them of their inalienable right to freedom, self-determination, and happiness!"

"In the wider world, education has been replaced by indoctrination! Basic truths are subverted and twisted, and thrust at the people on screens that invade every corner of their existence. The natural systems are disintegrating, the planet is choking under a cloud of carbon dioxide, and no one has the simple sense to regenerate the forests and plant more trees! Millions of people are displaced and homeless, living in makeshift squalor. The entire planet is on the verge of disaster!"

"Everywhere you look, the world is at war with itself, Mr Saomes. Wrongs must be righted! Falsehoods must be exposed and rectified. Social engineering must be undone. The faceless men and organisations of the ruling elite who manipulate every aspect for their own profit must be overthrown."

"To quote an old adage of warfare, there are never enough soldiers at the front. In the pursuit of justice there are always more battles to be fought! To you and to all I say, look at your armoury. What are your greatest strengths? What weapons do you possess, and in which struggle can you make the greatest difference?"

"Perhaps you could give thought to which battle you might join or which cause you might champion. Often we cannot expect to win when we fight alone, but sometimes we can change the outcome of a skirmish by throwing our weight behind others."

"There has never been a darker or more crucial time for positive action in human history than right now, Mr Saomes. The peoples of the world must be united, to speak with a common voice, to demand their governments abandon the scourge of Capitalism and the short-sightedness of a One World Government! Human happiness must be placed ahead of personal wealth and company profits."

"Countries must be rebuilt to become self-sufficient. Self-indulgence must be supplanted with self-restraint and self-mastery. Each and every person on earth has a marvellous potential that most will never know because the ways of the world continue to oppress and weigh them down. Choose a cause, find a target, and proceed to deploy your weapons wisely, Mr Saomes. The possibilities are endless!"

At the conclusion of his outburst, Mahonri was off to attend to his errand, and I was left shell-shocked. In a frantic burst of mental activity I began to consider my armoury as Mahonri had suggested. What weapons did I command that could make the slightest difference to a single soul?

I spent my day grappling with a myriad of thoughts and emotions. As night fell, I lay on my bunk staring at the sky. Visions flashed past my mind's eye like snippets of a newsreel. I reflected on my life and the many stories and articles I'd written over the years that had caused me to rise to prominence among the journalistic community. I recalled the places I'd visited and the people I'd interviewed in my desperate quest to uncover the real truth behind world events. Then I returned to the here and now, and to what I could only describe as the greatest story of all. But what was I to do with it? More to the point, what was I to do with me?

The full moon shone through the sky-window. I watched its steady journey from east to west until it was gone from view. As I beheld its magnificence, I felt conscious of my own insignificance. Could I really make a worthwhile difference in the world?

My thoughts drifted in the night, and I remembered back to an interview with a member of the scientific community. He appeared to be the typical mad scientist, wholly absorbed in some petty cause that no one else understood or cared about. The interview took place on a beautiful expanse of beach when the moon was full and high. Baby turtles were burrowing out of the dunes to make their awkward way to the water's edge. Birds swooped and carried off the young hatchlings by the thousands. And for those who managed to reach the water, other predators lined the shore and devoured thousands more.

The scientist was grabbing baby turtles by the twos and threes as quickly as he could and throwing them out to sea.

"Do you really think you can make a difference here?" the interviewer queried.

Without looking up, the scientist grabbed another small turtle and flung it to relative safety. "Well, I made a difference to that one!" he replied.

At the time I was young and I missed the point entirely. But right now, if I could be on that beach, I

too, would be pelting handfuls of turtles out to sea
with all the energy I could muster.

As the night deepened, the light of the moon
disappeared below the distant mountains, and the
stars hid behind heavy cloud. I lay awake, wrestling
with my emotions with such intensity I could barely
breathe. There had to be an answer to my dilemma—
but what?

At my lowest ebb, in the depths of darkness and
agony, I felt my heart tighten inside my heaving
chest. At that moment of deepest despair, I can only
suppose that I experienced something miraculous. My
swirling mind burst through the vale of blackness and
into the brilliant light as if the windows of Heaven
had opened upon me. Suddenly I was awash with
inspiration, filling my soul like gushing water into an
empty vessel as a warm feeling of surety pulsed at the
very core of my being. In an instant I knew I *could*
make a difference—that I *could* improve the world for
someone, if only I had the courage to try.

I realised that when I saw someone in need, I
could no longer turn away. I had to 'do something' to
help—to make the situation better! And even though
my contribution may be small, when supported by
others—together, we could bring about a tidal wave
of change.

I had always believed one man could not make a
difference, but now I could see how wrong I was. My

mistake was holding to the concept that we stand alone, that on our own we are powerless against injustice. One voice crying in the wilderness cannot move a mountain or hold up the sky. But a thousand voices—nay a million screeching banshees cannot go unnoticed for long! Often, all that is needed is a voice of hope, or someone to organise the troops and set a plan in motion.

In Yuwmah I learned that every man, woman, and child can make a difference to someone, especially to those less fortunate than themselves. If each of us could only find enough concern for those around us, and do something to make their load a little lighter or their journey more bearable—what a difference we could make! Every one of us can help change the world, one unselfish act at a time if only we have the mind and will to try.

As the sun rose, I reflected on Mahonri's words, but this time I had answers where before there were none. Weapons I had, and a sizeable arsenal! I was a journalist and writer. In the wider world, the pen is mightier than any sword, and the modern keyboard is far more lethal. My greatest problem had arisen because I'd misplaced or devalued the old 'me'. I'd left my past life behind—not realising the tremendous value and worth of who I once was.

I've always believed that the ability to read and write are the most powerful tools we have to change the course of history. In times past, my words were sort after by countless publishers who paid handsomely for a few idle comments! Even now, I had an international following at my fingertips! I could smite any foe, wherever they were in the world!

But more than this, I could disseminate information to those who might listen, to be as a beacon to those who wanted to know more. Perhaps I could motivate others who lived lives of disinterest, and encourage them to stand up for whatever they believed but had never cared enough to defend. The possibilities continued to flash through my mind, each one enormous and far-reaching.

Mahonri was right again. We cannot sit idly by and let evil flourish. If we are to be truly free, we must stand up for what we believe and push back the intrusions of the world, to regain control of our homes and lives.

I had come to understand that we are manipulated by an insidious system that is not of our making, and definitely not beneficial to our happiness or our betterment. Social engineering is prominent all around the world. The subtle demands to conform to a central norm can be overpowering. The people of the world must stand united against the faceless manipulators and take back our independence and our freedoms.

Yes, Mahonri was right again. There are never too many troops at the front! Everyone can make a contribution. We cannot afford to turn away, or close our eyes, or leave anything to others. The control of the many by the few must cease. Human happiness must become the central tenet of all we do and say if we are to have a better world.

I remember reading on the wall of the Great Library, "Evil will prosper when good men do nothing to expose its unholy face". From this point onward, I will be a good man and stand against evil wherever I find it. We can all make a difference, if only we would allow ourselves to try.

With my head held high I hurried off to find Mahonri. He observed me through knowing eyes as I approached.

"Ah, Mr Saomes! What a good morning it is. I see you have found your answers at last!" He jostled me as he shook my hand in congratulation. "And in doing so you have become reborn to new possibilities and a new life of purpose and meaning." His frail arm wrapped around my shoulders in a way that made me feel proud.

As we chatted, I rehearsed my plans for the future, and through the course of the day I made the necessary arrangements for my departure, retiring early that evening to pack my things and prepare. Finally, I stretched out on my bunk for one last night in Yuwmah before returning to the greater world, and the life and the future I had hidden from for so long.

The following afternoon found me sitting at the gathering place in pleasant conversation with Toosa. Moments later, I was surrounded by my closest friends enjoying a splendid farewell. Mahonri stood in our midst and stretched out his arms until the crowd came to order.

"Before Mr Saomes leaves us, I wish to say a few words on behalf of all here assembled." he began.

"Your transformation is almost complete, Mr Saomes," came Mahonri's smiling approval. "But if you would permit me the honour, there are two things I wish to bestow upon you before you depart. I would first like to give you a parting gift."

As he spoke, he removed the string of beads from around his neck and gestured to place them over my head. Instinctively, and out of deep respect I dropped to one knee and bowed politely. The beads settled heavily upon me as Mahonri's hand rested firmly on my shoulder. As I moved to stand, he stepped behind me, placing his right hand on top of my head to hold me down. With a nod, the other men came forward, each placing their right hand on top of Mahonri's, and their left hand on the shoulder of the man next to them, forming an unbroken circle around me.

At that moment I felt a flow of energy surging through the crown of my head, infusing every cell of my body. By the power of that energy, I felt strangely cleansed and purified. My mind was rejuvenated and quickened, and I'm sure my face shone and my whole body glowed.

Mahonri began to speak with a voice like thunder, calling me by name. He spoke with such power; I shuddered with every utterance. I can still remember the words and visions etched forever into the fabric of my mind. His final supplication was the most memorable and inspiring of all.

"Mr Saomes, it has been said of the Yuwmahn people that, 'they move among us and influence our world for good; yet we know not who they are or from whence they come. They are as the invisible ones, for they show themselves only to those who need to see' You, Mr Saomes, have become one of us—a fellow Yuwmahn. I therefore bestow upon you the mantle of courage and strength, of humility, and invisibility, and I beseech you to go and do as Yuwmahns have done for centuries: to earnestly strive to make the world better, to fight for right, to stand against injustice, to defend the weak, to lift up the down-trodden; to encourage, inspire and promote that which is good, virtuous, right and true. Become as a light unto the world, that by your efforts, others may see their way through the darkness and find eternal love and happiness."

Evening found me sitting on my swag at the edge of our makeshift runway. Once again I was dressed in my western clothes. On the outside I was slimmer, stronger, and healthier. On the inside I was transformed into a new being; my soul had enlarged manyfold and my mind had matured and grown a thousand years.

Through the course of my time in Yuwmah I was drawn into the Yuwmahn way, to become a willing accomplice to their every aspiration. In short, the 'me' now sitting here was a different person than 'he' who had arrived, and I had no doubt as to which was the better man.

I looked down at the footprints my heavy boots had made on the damp grass, and my eyes traced them back towards the deep valley beyond. Each of those footprints would fade in the morning sun, wiping away the last remaining witness that I was ever here. Yet the will and desire within me to fulfil the charge of my Yuwmahn commission would never be erased. My future mission and purpose were clear: to do all within my power to improve our world for every living creature—and in doing so, to find my own unique pathway to the greatest happiness of all.

POSTSCRIPT

I feel it a fitting gesture to close with
Mahonri's parting words:

"May your journey be filled with the fruits of wisdom;
may you choose that which brings you and yours the
greatest joy in abundance—and may you share that
joy wherever you go."

ABOUT JOHN SAOMES

John Saomes is an Australian author and poet whose books and novels follow the central theme of 'making the world a better place'. His writing promotes thought and discussion about the kind of world we desire most, with emphasis on enhancing human happiness and maximising the human experience.

John lives in the beautiful hinterland of Australia's Gold Coast. He champions global initiatives to promote and uphold personal rights and freedoms and efforts to build a better and fairer world for all.

Sign up for your free ebook
and join the Yuwmahn Revolution at:

www.johnsaomes.com

BOOKS BY JOHN SAOMES

From The Yuwmahn Compendium
Journey to Yuwmah
Return to Yuwmah

Poetry
The Days of Dinkum Dodger - Volume I
The Days of Dinkum Dodger - Volume II
The Days of Dinkum Dodger - Volume III

UPCOMING BOOKS BY JOHN SAOMES

From The Yuwmahn Compendium
Seven Conversations of Happiness

Poetry
For Love of Woman
For Love of Fellow Man
For Love of Life